HIDDEN DANGER

A SMALL-TOWN GUARDIANS NOVEL

Jennifer Pierce

Hidden Danger
By Jennifer Pierce
© Copyright 2018 Jennifer Pierce

Published by Anaiah Romance
An imprint of Anaiah Press, LLC.
7780 49th ST N. #129
Pinellas Park, FL 33781

First Anaiah Romance print edition June 2018
Edited by Kara Leigh Miller
Book Design by Eden Plantz
Cover Design by Laura Heritage

www.anaiahpress.com

To my father, Bob Dale. You are greatly missed.

Acknowledgements

Thank you to my Lord and Savior, for His mercy and grace. To Him be the glory.

Acknowledgements are hard. There are so many people I credit for helping me along the way. Thank you!

To my husband, Sam Pierce, for being supportive during this journey.

To my children, you can accomplish anything if you put your mind to it.

To my mother, Wilma Dale, for believing in me and watching my children so I can meet those deadlines.

To my best friend, Aaron Lee. Thanks for cheering me on and pushing me to finish.

To Jessica Bailey for talking me into doing NaNoWriMo one year, even though neither of us finished. Did we actually start?

To all my friends and family that helped with advice, critiquing, and brainstorming.

planned the repairs and to-do list down to the last minute of her stay. She'd been counting on her brother, Jacob, to help, but he'd been called away on a job for the security company he worked for, pushing back her timeline by at least a week. Honestly, it had hardly come as a surprise. In the two years since his wife had died, he'd buried himself in work, taking every job they'd give him.

Staring with dismay at the red paint, she mentally calculated the extra cleanup effort. The good news was that the house had needed to be repainted anyway. She would just need to add time for a couple coats of primer.

The driver slowed to a stop and put the car in park. Once again, she wished she could have driven to Whitehaven instead of taking the bus. She needed a new car. Hers never would have made the drive, and it would cost more to fix than to buy a new one. She had a nice down payment saved up but had decided to wait until after the summer. Instead, she would put her money into the house and recoup it after the sale.

She got out of the taxi and met the driver by the trunk. He pulled her suitcase out and set it on the ground. She handed him the fare and grabbed the handle of her suitcase, pulling it to the porch steps. She climbed the steps and hesitated at the front door. Her chest tightened with anxiety.

It had been three months since her father had died, and she missed him so much. She'd agreed to come home during summer vacation to help Jacob go through their dad's stuff to get the house cleaned up to go on the market. But she wasn't ready to step back into the house, to see the memories of her mother and father in every corner. Sliding the key in the door and unlocking it, she pushed it open and was greeted by the stale smell of an old, unoccupied house. She hung her keys on the nail by the front door.

Glancing around the living room was like stepping back into her childhood. It hadn't changed in the six years since she'd left for college. At first, after the way high school had ended, coming home

ONE

The driveway was marked by a lone wooden post, adorned with a beautiful hand-painted mailbox—or it had been the last time Maggie Jones had been in Whitehaven. As the tax turned in the long driveway to the old family house, the twiste remains came into view. She had once spent hours painting ar repainting that box until she'd deemed it perfect. She'd paint their last name in the center and surrounded it by intricat designed flowers. The same flowers that had grown in her moth garden. Her parents had been so proud of that mailbox. Now, it nothing but a heap of metal laying crumpled on the ground. winced at the sight of it.

"Kids." The disgust in the taxi driver's voice made Ma smile. "Too much time on their hands these days."

"I talked to my brother a couple of days ago, and he didn anything about it. They must have done it after he left town."

The taxi continued up the drive. Once past the scrubby she could see the words *ARE YOU READY?* painted in bloc letters on the front of the house. Her heart raced. What was on?

She agreed with the taxi driver about the mailbox. Af there wasn't much to do in a small rural area like Whiteha\ cause trouble. She wasn't so sure a drunken stunt could exp red words though.

She couldn't tear her gaze from the front of the hous done a walkthrough after her father's funeral in Marcl for visits had been hard. Gradually, the pain had eased. Now that both of her parents had passed, her ties to the town were gone and selling the house would be a relief.

She found the keys to the truck in the rolltop desk her father had kept next to the fireplace. Locking the front door behind her, she walked around the property looking for any other signs of vandalism. She didn't find any, and, relieved, she moved toward the garage where the old truck would be.

The truck door squeaked in protest as she opened it. The beast, as she had called it when she was learning to drive, was old and beat up, but it had always purred when started. She climbed in and turned the key. Nothing. She tried again. It sputtered and then died. *One more time, come on, baby.* She turned the key again, and it roared to life. So much for purring. Perhaps because it hadn't been started in a couple of months.

Twenty minutes later, she pulled into the parking lot of the sheriff's office. She hadn't seen a need to call an officer out to the house. The sheriff's department was small and only had a handful of deputies. This wasn't a life-or-death emergency.

CJ Rogers had been the sheriff as long as she could remember, and his name still emblazoned the department door. A blast of cool air washed over her when she opened it. The waiting room was empty save for one man sitting in a chair, his back to her, reading a magazine. There was no one at the desk, and she tapped the bell a couple of times to announce her presence.

"Well, if it isn't little Magpie Jones. The prodigal daughter returns," an unforgettable southern drawl announced from behind her. She'd know that voice anywhere. The voice that used to bring comfort now only angered her. She spun around, the last man she wanted to see occupied the waiting room seat.

"Well, if it isn't the heartbreaking Cody Smith. I should have known I'd meet you at the sheriff's office. It was only a matter of time before you were on the wrong side of the law." Her words held the pent-up anger she'd thought she'd released a long time ago.

"Now, Magpie, don't be like that." Cody furrowed his brows.

"Don't you Magpie me. You know how much I hate that name. My name is Maggie." She crossed her arms over her chest.

"May I help you?" asked a small voice from the reception desk behind her. Without another word, she turned her attention to the woman.

"Yes, ma'am, I need to see the sheriff about my father's, um, my land. Is he in?"

The woman looked at her and then sent a questioning look to Cody. She must have heard their conversation. Maggie's face was on fire, whether it was from embarrassment or from reliving the hurt and anger Cody had caused, she wasn't sure. Maybe it was both.

The receptionist finally responded, "He is in, but I don't know if he'll be able to see you." She looked past Maggie and straight at him. "Well, Sheriff? Are you available to speak with the lady?"

The floor fell out from under her. She took deep breaths, trying to process what the woman said. On her second inhale, Cody's favorite woodsy cologne filled her nostrils. In her shock, she hadn't heard him walk over to stand behind her.

Memories of their summer together crashed around her. Long walks hand in hand. Talking until the wee hours of the morning.

"Are you okay?" Concern filled his eyes.

"You're the sheriff?" Her voice squeaked. "But the door still says CJ Rogers."

"Here's the thing, Magpie—I'm sorry, *Maggie*—there weren't a lot of extra funds to change it until recently. We're getting it done next week actually."

For a moment, the pain of his rejection was pushed aside by those happy memories. Suddenly, all she wanted was a comforting hug, someone to lean on. When her mother had died, he had been

4

her rock. She needed that now. That need almost outweighed the hurt he had caused years ago.

Once upon a time, he had been her rock. But now? The idea of coming to Cody for any kind of help was intolerable. She didn't want to stand there, to be near him. "I can't do this. I shouldn't have come here anyway. Forget it. Thank you, Ms.—" She turned back to the receptionist.

"Dee, my name is Dee."

"Thank you, Dee. I'm sorry to have bothered you." She turned around and strode out the door.

"Maggie, wait!" he called from behind her. She kept walking to the truck. She wanted to put as much distance between the two of them as quickly as she could.

"Maggie, come on. Stop and talk to me."

She turned around and threw her hand in the air to stop him from coming any closer. "Don't. Just don't."

She turned back and continued her march to the old beat up truck. She climbed in and slammed the door, praying it would start because she couldn't let him see the moisture welling up in her eyes.

She drove back to the house with tears blurring her vision. Coming in contact with Cody, having to talk to him, had unsettled her and only added to the thoughts and emotions she had going on. How could one person be the cause of so much joy and so much pain simultaneously?

Seeing the red painted words again added to her current dismal mood. What had she done to deserve this? Whitehaven was the last place she wanted to be. She'd only come back to help Jacob with the house, and within hours of returning, she'd come face to face with the reason she had run six years ago.

Once she was inside, she grabbed the newest novel she had gotten in the mail and headed straight for the bathroom. She hadn't had dinner, but she was in no mood to eat. Maybe a long soak in a hot bath would ease some of the pain that she was revisiting.

The house phone rang, interrupting her before she could make it up the stairs. She quickly turned around and grabbed the cordless phone from the end table.

"Hello?"

"Maggie, this is—"

Instantly recognizing the voice on the other end, she said, "I know who it is. What do you want?"

"Maggie, I know you came to the office today for some sort of problem with the land. Please talk to me about what's going on."

"There is nothing to talk about with you. I'll figure it out on my own." She hung up before he had a chance to speak.

The phone rang again. *Persistent, isn't he?* She let it keep ringing and climbed the stairs to her childhood room. The ringing stopped, and the answering machine picked up. Her father had refused to embrace the twenty-first century. She gathered her robe and toiletries and headed for the bathroom. She turned on some music on her cell phone.

She stayed in the bath until the water turned cold, taking advantage of the only free time she'd have before the end of summer. Tomorrow, she'd start work. She climbed from the tub completely relaxed and toweled off in her bedroom. The phone rang again while she dressed in her favorite rubber ducky pajamas and matching slippers. She rolled her eyes and descended the stairs to the kitchen. She needed a hot cup of tea.

She glanced at the blinking light on the answering machine as she placed a cup of water in the microwave. Two messages. Maybe Sheriff Heartbreaker did get the hint. Pushing the play button, she steeled herself for whatever he had to say.

"Maggie, it's Cody. Please answer the phone." There was a pause. If he had expected her to pick up the call, he had been sadly mistaken. "I'm heading out your way. See you in a few."

The next message clicked on. "Maggie, you definitely need to report the vandalism. Even if it is just kids screwing around, the

6

message is threatening... I know you're home. I knocked. I guess you're ignoring me... Listen, if you won't talk to me, will you at least talk to one of the deputies? I'll send Deputy Grainger out tomorrow morning. Believe it or not, I just want to help." He paused again. "I'm here for you."

Sure, he'd be there for her. He'd said that six years ago too. But then he'd left her standing alone in a cloud of dust as he drove away. Cody was the last person she wanted to talk to or get help from.

She pictured her father's vandalized mailbox and the words splashed on the house. Much as she wanted someone to look into it, she would not be asking him for help. She'd find help some other way, if she really needed it. Maggie deleted the messages and started to walk back to the kitchen table when the phone rang again. She exhaled a huff of annoyance and answered impatiently. "Hello?"

Heavy breathing filled the speaker. Had Cody pocket dialed her? "Are you ready to play a game?" The sound of the digitized voice sent chills racing up her spine. "Let's start with your boyfriend in the driveway. One for sorrow." A dial tone quickly replaced the dead air.

A sense of dread filled her. Who was that, and what was he talking about? A boyfriend in her driveway? She walked over to the window and cautiously peered out into the dusky yard. There was someone out there in a cruiser, all right. Cody. She hadn't thought he would still be sitting in her driveway.

Running to the front door, she yanked it open and shouted his name.

TWO

Her yell jolted Cody from his thoughts as Maggie came racing out of the house. Jumping from his car, he met her by the front door in seconds. The distinct crack of a gunshot split the crisp June night air. The sound of wood splintering and the sting of his bicep confirmed that something had hit the porch railing to his right. His heart raced, and his fight-or-flight instincts kicked in. He grabbed Maggie by the waist and pulled her through the front door, slamming it and sliding the deadbolt.

"Maggie, get down." He waved her to the area in front of the couch and pulled his sidearm from the holster on his belt. It was a good thing he had come straight from work. He turned off the lights and knelt below the window by the front door to keep an eye out for danger. "What made you come out screaming?"

"Someone called. A creepy machine voice asked if I wanted to play a game. He knew you were in the driveway." The fear in her voice was audible. "Someone is watching the house."

"Okay, stay there while I call for back up." Pulling his cell from his pocket, he hit the speed dial number for dispatch and turned his attention back to the yard.

"Dee, this is Sheriff Smith. I am at 1405 County Road 12, shots have been fired, and I'm in need of assistance. Dispatch a K9 unit as well." He put the phone down by his side and looked at Maggie.

She was doing what he had told her, sitting in the shadows, huddling herself up against the base of the couch, mouthing silent words as she clung to the cross around her neck. If memory served correctly, that was the cross her mother had given her for her eighteenth birthday, right before she passed away. Maggie had once told him that no matter how she was feeling, she would pray and the peace of God would descend on her. She would cling to that cross in her deepest prayers. He had always admired her faith. Was she praying for their safety now?

Cody turned his attention back to the window. It was dark out. He couldn't tell where the shot had originated, other than from behind his car. He'd wait for reinforcements and then start looking for the shooter. His immediate priority was keeping Maggie safe until his deputies arrived.

Maggie sat on the floor in ducky pajamas and matching slippers, fear and confusion emanating from her features. All he wanted to do was gather her in his arms and tell her he'd do anything to keep her safe. But he couldn't do that now. If he let down his guard, whoever was shooting at them could get the upper hand. Besides, her reaction to him this afternoon made it perfectly clear that she would not welcome his attention.

He kept a constant lookout, scanning for any moving shadows and listening for any unusual noises that might indicate someone was encroaching on the house.

"Cody?" Maggie's gentle voice pulled his focus from the window. She was squinting at him in the dim light. "Are you bleeding? Were you shot?" She moved to get up, but he motioned her to stay where she was.

He looked down at his arm. The constant stinging hadn't let him forget that he had been hit by something, but he couldn't focus on his injuries yet. There hadn't been another shot since the first one, but he didn't want to test the waters.

"Relax, Magpie. It's only a scratch. I'll live." He gave her what he hoped was a reassuring smile. Sirens reached his ears before the red flashing lights came into view. *Finally, backup has arrived.* One cruiser pulled into the drive and screeched to a halt yards from the front steps.

"Maggie, stay here while I go talk to my deputy." Unlocking the deadbolt, he opened the door and scanned the porch. Once the area was secured, he and Maggie needed to talk.

He stepped out onto the lit porch, every muscle in his body tensed, waiting for another shot. Deputy Grainger met him at the bottom of the porch steps and then followed him to his car.

"There was a single shot from somewhere on the other side of my car. We'll need to search the area. Dee is supposed to be sending out the K9 unit, as well. Once they're here we can see if there's a trail."

As he finished updating Grainger, three more cruisers pulled in, Deputy McKinley in the lead. Deputy Peters and his K9 partner, Luna, followed, and Deputy Minton was the last. They exited their cruisers and walked toward him waiting on his instructions.

"Grainger. You, McKinley, Peters, and Luna secure the perimeter. See if Luna can get a scent of whoever was here. Minton, I heard the bullet hit the railing on the porch. Grab your evidence kit and see what you can find."

The front door opened, and Maggie stepped out on to the porch. He jogged to her. *How am I going to protect her if she isn't going to listen?*

"Maggie, what are you doing out here?" *Does she not realize someone just took a shot at her? For all we know he's still out there watching.* "We haven't finished canvassing the area. This is a crime scene. Go back inside until everything is cleared."

"This is my father's property, and someone is targeting me. I want to know who and why." Maggie's defiant eyes dared him to argue.

How he'd missed those big, beautiful, green eyes. There was a time he thought he would get to look into those eyes every day for the rest of his life. *No. You did what was necessary, what was best for Maggie, no matter how much it hurt.*

She looked away and waved her hand in the direction of the deputies. "Besides, now that the cavalry is here, I really don't think anyone would be stupid enough to hang around. I'm not going to let anyone scare me away."

Her stubborn streak was cute when they were younger, but right now she was playing with fire. He set his jaw.

"Listen, Maggie—"

"Sheriff, come take a look at this," Deputy Minton interrupted. Cody walked the few feet to where Minton was crouched. Maggie was right on his heels, like when they were kids.

He followed Minton's gaze to a small cloth square lying on the porch not far from the front door. Cody pulled his multipurpose tool from his pocket, squatted down in front of the object, and used the plier tool to move it. It was a beanbag. Written in small block letters were the words *one for sorrow.* Their shooter hadn't been shooting to kill. He was trying to scare Maggie. The note gave him an alarming sense of déjà vu, sending his thoughts back to the first case he'd worked after being elected sheriff.

"*One for sorrow.* That's what the caller said." Maggie's soft voice echoed from behind him.

"It looks like it ricocheted off the porch column, splintering a portion of it, and landed here," Deputy Minton informed them, pointing out the trajectory the beanbag had taken.

So, the splintered wood was what had hit him as he had grabbed Maggie. "Bag it. Maybe we can get something useful off it," he directed toward Minton, then turned to Maggie. "We need to talk." He placed his hand on her forearm and led her to the front door.

She abruptly pulled her arm from his grasp. "Yes, Sheriff, I suppose we do." She turned on the lights and headed to the kitchen, leaving him standing in the living room.

12

"You can still call me Cody. You didn't have a problem doing so about thirty minutes ago." He leaned against the kitchen island.

"Okay. Talk."

"First and foremost, please tell me those are not the same duck slippers Jake bought you for Christmas when you were fifteen." He tried to lighten the mood. She was already dealing with the loss of her father. She didn't need this craziness piled on top of it.

Her face blushed. Was she surprised that he would remember those slippers? "No, they are not. Now onto official business or you may leave."

"Can you tell me what happened up until you came out on the porch hollering?"

"You had called me. After I hung up, I gathered my stuff for a bath. The phone rang again. I assumed it was you, so I ignored it." She reached into the cabinet, pulled out a thermos and filled it with fresh coffee from the maker. She must have started a pot after he'd gone out to investigate.

"After my bath, I came down and saw that I had two messages, so I checked them. I was walking away when the phone rang again. You know the rest." She grabbed several coffee cups from the shelf and set them in front of Cody. He placed his hand over hers. Her hand was as soft as he remembered.

"Magpie, listen." He softened his voice.

She yanked her hand from his, "Cody, please don't. I can't do this." Tears pooled in her eyes. "Here's some coffee and cups. Take them to your men." She turned and quickly walked from the kitchen.

Picking up the thermos and tray of cups, he went back out to his officers. There was work to do now. Maybe a couple more days would calm her emotions.

As he walked out the front door, one of the deputies signaled to him. Hoping they had a lead and could wrap this up quickly, he set the cups and thermos on the hood of one of the squad cars. "Ms.

13

Jones was gracious enough to provide coffee. Tell me what you found."

Deputies Grainger and McKinley ambled up. Deputy Grainger was the first to speak. "We searched the area to the north until we got to the road. We couldn't find anything. There wasn't a car parked on the road as we came in, so I doubt our shooter escaped that way. We circled around and searched the woods surrounding the house. There's a small creek about a quarter of the mile to the south. Luna seemed to pick up a small trail there but then got confused and kept running us in circles."

"So, other than the bean bag, and the broken wood on the porch, we don't have any evidence?" *Except the ache in my arm.* "Whoever this guy is, he's good, and he knows the area. Okay, do one more sweep of the woods, and I'll make sure the outside of the house is secure."

He walked the outside perimeter with a flashlight, inspecting every visible inch. All the windows were intact, and there was no evidence of anyone being around the windows or the back door. He checked the detached garage, and it was secure as well. He slowly climbed the porch steps with Deputy McKinley right behind him and knocked on the door. Maggie's exhausted voice invited him in. She lay cuddled on the couch with a book. Her auburn hair was disheveled, and her eyes were tired.

"Maggie, we canvassed the area and couldn't find anything or anyone. I want a deputy to check all the interior doors and windows of the house as a precaution. Would that be okay?"

She nodded her consent. He turned and nodded to Deputy McKinley.

"Has anything else weird or unusual happened since you've been back in Whitehaven?"

He listened as she told him about the damaged mailbox and the vandalism. He couldn't figure out who would want to target her in any way, much less a motive for doing so. He made a mental note to call the security agency and see if they could reach Jake. He didn't want Maggie alone and, knowing her, she would refuse any help he tried to offer.

Deputy McKinley joined them in the living room. "The house is secure, sir. All windows and exterior doors are locked."

Cody nodded at McKinley, who returned the nod before exiting the house.

"Magpie, what happened tonight is an indication that someone doesn't want you here. I don't think it would be wise for you to stay here alone until we can find out who did this. Please consider staying somewhere else until we do."

She stood with an air of frustration, tossing the covers and book to the side. "You and your deputies have been here for hours, and you just said the area was secure. It's late, and there's no sense in me trying to get a hotel at this time. I think I'll be fine."

"If that's what you want. I'll have a deputy stationed outside for the rest of the night. If you need anything else, anything at all, please call the office. I understand you don't want to have anything to do with me but don't let your stubborn streak put you in harm's way." He walked out the door, and she closed it behind him. He didn't move until she secured the deadbolt.

THREE

The ringing of the house phone woke Maggie from much needed sleep. She stretched and looked at the clock on the mantel—8:30 a.m. She must have finally been exhausted enough to let sleep consume her. After the mysterious caller last night, she was almost afraid to answer the phone. *I'm not going to let this creep win. He will not scare me into hiding.*

"Hello?" Did she really sound that shaky?

"Ms. Jones, this is Gary at Pete's Hardware. I thought I would call and let you know the paint you ordered is in."

Relief washed over her. She'd ordered basic white paint over the phone from home, knowing her father and his lack of upkeep would mean the whole house, inside and outside, would need painted. "Thank you, Gary. I'm going to be in town later this morning. I'll pick it up then. I'm also going to need an exterior primer. Do you have any in stock?"

"Let me check. I'm going to put you on hold for a sec, okay?"

Tacky hold music started playing on his side of the line.

The house and surrounding area had finally been cleared, and Cody and the deputies had departed around two o'clock in the morning. After they left, a feeling of unease had enveloped her. Even though there had been a deputy stationed outside, she'd been suspicious of every sound.

She'd gone to her father's room and found his pistol exactly where he had always kept it. Though she hadn't shot a gun since he had taken her and Jacob to the gun range when she was fourteen, it had brought her some peace of mind.

But the biggest comfort had come from her Bible. She had begun reading in Proverbs. Chapter eighteen, verse ten resonated with her. *The name of the Lord is a strong tower. The righteous run to it and are safe.*

"Maggie? We do have some primer. I'll put it with your exterior paint. Are you going to need any other painting supplies?"

"I'm going to have to look and see what dad has lying around. I'll make a list and pick it all up later. Thank you so much."

"You're very welcome, and I'll see you later."

She placed the cordless phone on a charging station in the living room and headed to the kitchen for breakfast. The cabinets were pretty bare, but she remembered seeing a granola bar in one of them. She'd have to get some groceries while she was in town.

Grabbing a notebook and pen from the junk drawer in the kitchen, she took her granola bar to the table to make a list of things that needed to be added to her to-do list. The first thing on that list was the red mess.

A knock at her front door interrupted her train of thought. She set her granola bar down and walked to the living room.

Before she reached the door, there was another knock. "Margaret, it's Amelia from church."

Her former youth leader? That was a surprise. She hurriedly opened the door. Before Maggie had a chance to welcome Amelia, she'd grabbed her and smothered her in one of her famous bear hugs.

"This was on your porch when I pulled up." Amelia handed Maggie a small white box

"Amelia, what on earth are you doing here?" She took the box and invited Amelia into the house.

"Jacob told me you'd be in town this month. I'm still the youth leader, and I'm teaching the youth about service. What better way to teach it than to put it into action?" Amelia gave a small shrug.

"My condolences on your father. I'm so sorry I wasn't able to make it to the funeral. We were on a mission trip, and I didn't even know he had passed until we returned. I really wish I could have been here for you." She reached out and grabbed Maggie's hand. "But I can be here for you now. Why don't you let our youth help around with the things you need done? I see painting will be a priority."

Maggie set the box on the coffee table and gestured for Amelia to have a seat next to her on the couch. Amelia had always been a helper. She had a servant's spirit, as Maggie's mother would put it. She was always the first to volunteer when work needed to be done. When her mother had died seven years ago, Amelia had baked a casserole for them every other night for a month. She'd been a shoulder to cry on, an ear to listen, and had wisdom beyond her years.

Maggie had missed her. After she left Whitehaven, she had kept in touch with Amelia through email but eventually that stopped. She'd gotten so busy with school and writing. She'd come home to visit her dad all the time, but she'd never left the house. Dad always had everything she needed.

"Thank you for the offer, but I don't have the supplies yet. I'll be heading into town later to pick them up. Plus, I don't know if you heard, but there was an incident here last night. Kind of a creepy thing—someone was watching the house, trying to scare me. No one was hurt, it's probably nothing more than a joke, but I'd rather the youth not be here in case there is a real threat." Not to mention the fact that allowing a bunch of juveniles to paint could be disastrous. No. She'd do the painting, make sure it was done right. They needed the house to sell quickly.

"Oh, no! I hadn't heard. Thank God no one was hurt." She closed her eyes and looked heavenward. "Well, we'll put off having the youth come, but maybe I can get some of the adults to help. Since I'm here, tell me what's new in your world."

"There's not a lot to tell. I went to college, graduated, and now I work as an elementary school librarian." Maggie turned more toward Amelia, and brought her leg up, lacing her foot under her other leg.

"Any special fellows in your life? Cody's still single, you know." Amelia wiggled her eyebrows.

"No. No special man. And Cody Smith is in the past. *Not* a mistake to be made again."

Amelia placed her hand on Maggie's knee. "You know, back in youth group, he'd always been a handful. Causing all kinds of ruckus and chasing the girls. Until that summer your momma died that is. He changed that summer. You two may have been able to fool everyone else, but I knew you were seeing each other. You're the reason he changed, you know."

"I'm not sure what you mean." Maggie's neck heated. She didn't think anyone had known about their relationship.

"Oh, honey. That boy was head over heels for you. Even after you left. He moped around like a sad puppy. He's been single ever since."

If Amelia was right, why had he broken up with her? If he'd really loved her, why would he cause so much pain?

The phone rang, saving her from having the conversation about how her relationship ended. She grabbed the phone from its cradle. "Hello."

"Maggie. Good thing I caught you." Gary's voice echoed over the line. "I know I told you this morning that we had some exterior primer, but I didn't realize it was on hold."

Maggie put her hand over the receiver. "It's Gary from the hardware store. I'll be just a minute."

"No worries. I need to be going anyway. I'll see myself out." Amelia reached across the couch and gave her a hug before leaving.

"That's all right, Gary. Can we order some?"

"That we can, but it will be a couple days before we can get it in. The order for this week's first truck has already been sent in."

"That's fine. I'm in no hurry." In reality, she was. She didn't want to have to keep staring at the words scrawled across her house, but she also didn't have the time to drive to neighboring towns to see if they had what she needed.

"Good. Good."

"I'm going to make that list of supplies and still come get them and the paint today though."

"I'll see you later then."

She hung up the phone and walked to the kitchen to make an inventory of her painting supplies. She started singing her favorite hymn, "Victory in Jesus," while she dug through the kitchen supply closet. She started with her favorite verse, the one about angels singing and the old redemption story.

She stacked the supplies she could find on an old paint tray, and she turned to put them on the island when a man standing in her doorway startled her. She yelped, dropping the tray and scattering everything across the floor.

"Sorry to startle you. I was about to knock on the door when Amelia opened it. She said you were on the phone. I knocked and called your name, but you didn't answer. Now I know why."

The cadence of her heart started to slow when she recognized Cody. How long had he been standing there staring at her? She took a moment to take in his handsome figure leaning against the doorframe, his hands in his jeans' pockets. Memories of them together in that same kitchen years ago slowly crept into her mind.

"What can I help you with today, Sheriff?" She bent over to pick up the mess. Cody stepped into the kitchen and bent over to help. His presence filled the room. Her breath hitched as if there wasn't enough air. They piled everything onto the tray she had been holding. As he took the tray from her, his hand rested on hers. Warmth radiated up her arm, threatening to go straight to her heart, but she snatched her hand away, not daring to feel anything more. He set the tray on the counter and she turned away quickly, unwilling to look at him. Buying time, she walked to the sink and washed her hands. She dried her hands on a kitchen towel before turning her attention to the tray on the counter. Studiously ignoring him, she started laying things out to take inventory before her trip into town.

"I came back for some follow-up questions about last night's incident." He stood next to her and helped her organize the painting supplies. His close proximity was all she could focus on.

"I already know about the mailbox and the paint incidents that led up to last night. Can you think of anything that had happened prior to those? Even anything months ago? Maybe your dad had mentioned weird things going on around the property?"

"I can't think of anything out of the ordinary. He talked about the usual problems, you know, wild animals getting into the trash, the neighbor's dog finding his way to the house. Dad would have to call Mrs. Brown to come get him." She retreated to the kitchen table to retrieve her notebook and pen, diligently making her list to avoid looking at Cody. She would need to get a couple more rollers and some masking tape.

His cologne wafted toward her. She closed her eyes and took a deep breath. He still wore the same brand. In that instant, she remembered every embrace, resting her head on his chest, breathing in that wonderful scent that was always concentrated there. He'd once confessed to intentionally spraying it there after she'd told him how much she loved it.

She needed more space between them to clear her head. She walked into the living room, leaving Cody in the kitchen. The white box on the coffee table caught her eye. She'd forgotten about it.

"What about before you came back to Whitehaven? Did anything suspicious happen to you? Have you been threatened before?" Cody called from the kitchen.

She wasn't going to be able to avoid him as long as he had questions about last night. Reluctantly, she took the box back to the kitchen and laid it on the island. The quicker she answered his questions the sooner he'd leave. He'd made himself comfortable at the kitchen table while she'd been in the living room.

"No, nothing. I live a quiet life. I'm an elementary school librarian."

"A librarian? I thought you moved off to college in pursuit of a writing career?"

"Well, things change. When I'm not working at the school, I tutor at the Boys and Girls Club and outreach center during the week. When I have free time, I write."

Maggie gave the box a frown. She wasn't expecting any deliveries here in Whitehaven. It was about time for her monthly book order to come in. Perhaps her neighbor had been nice enough to somehow forward them. This wasn't the typical box they came in, though, and she hadn't thought the mail delivered out here. Her father had had a post office box for as long as she could remember. The mailbox had been more of a way to mark their drive than to actually collect the mail.

She retrieved some scissors from the utensil drawer and cut the tape holding the lid in place. She laid the scissors to the side and removed the lid. Inside the box, cradled in white tissue paper lay a black jewelry box. She opened the box, and the hair on the back of her neck prickled as nausea roiled in her stomach.

No. It can't be.

FOUR

Maggie's face had lost all color. Cody got a glimpse of a small, black box before she dropped it and ran from the room.

"Maggie? What is it?"

He crossed to the island and picked up the box. Nestled inside were two ornate wedding rings.

He furrowed his brows. When he had talked to Maggie last night about her life she hadn't mentioned a husband, past or present. Was Maggie married? Did she have a boyfriend who had asked her to marry him?

A loud thump came from the second floor followed by a muffled cry. Dropping the box, Cody ran toward the stairs. As he climbed the steps, he cautiously unholstered his service weapon.

"Maggie?" He listened for any sound. Hearing a quiet sniffle come from the right, he tiptoed in the direction of the room, keeping a vigilant eye of his surroundings. He'd been in the Jones' house enough times to know that the crying was coming from Maggie's parents' room. He stopped at the door and slowly peeked around the doorframe.

The room was pristine except the contents of several jewelry boxes dumped on the floral bedspread. Maggie sat on the floor in front of the bed, her head in her hands.

He holstered his weapon and knelt in front of her. "Maggie? What's going on?"

She lifted her head and looked at him. Tears ran down her cheeks. She grabbed a small, wooden jewelry box and showed it to him. "After my mom died, dad bought this box and kept her ring in it. He would come to the room and just look at the ring. When he died, we took his wedding ring and put it in the box with mom's."

He reached out and wiped away a tear rolling down her cheek.

"I'm missing something. Are the rings in that box downstairs from a boyfriend? Is there something you want to talk about?" His heart constricted at the thought of Maggie marrying someone else. But, even as he asked his questions, he logically dismissed them. A set of wedding rings from a boyfriend shouldn't upset her the way these had. Not unless they maybe came from an aggressive ex or something. But how would that connect to her parents? It didn't make sense.

His mind lingered on the rings. He'd once hoped that he would be the one to give her a wedding ring. He shook the thought off. He'd ended his chances for a happily ever after with her years ago.

"No, Cody. Look." She handed him an empty little wooden box. "The rings in the box downstairs are my parents' rings. I knew it as soon as I saw them. This note was in their box up here."

She handed Cody a folded piece of paper. *Two for joy.* That sense of déjà vu from last night returned. It was almost like the first case he had handled as sheriff. Another woman taunted with notes.

Iris's case still haunted him. It probably would for the rest of his life. He'd need to talk to Grainger and give him the option to recuse himself. If this was the same guy now as it was before, then Grainger was too close to this. Maggie took a shuddering breath, reclaiming his attention.

"Are you gonna be okay?" Her eyes met his, and he could tell she wanted to say no. She blinked away the moisture that threatened to escape and stood up.

Reaching out and placing a hand on her shoulder, he said, "Maggie, however the rings got into that box downstairs, I will figure it out."

Her shoulder tensed under his hand, almost like she was repulsed by his touch. He pulled his hand back. He knew he had hurt her, but he hadn't thought it would leave such a resounding effect six years later. He wanted to gather her in his arms and explain himself. To tell her how much he'd loved her then and how much he still did. Now was not the time. He needed to focus on finding out who was targeting Maggie and why. He couldn't let his feelings interfere with his job.

He followed her downstairs and into the kitchen. She pulled a pair of latex gloves from underneath the sink and handed them to Cody. "I'm sure you'll want these. Amelia said the box was on the porch when she showed up this morning about eight forty-five."

He took the gloves and put them on. He picked up the lid and looked for a postmark or anything indicating that the package was delivered by a packaging service. There wasn't one. Someone had put the package on Maggie's porch. And there was a good chance that whoever had left the package may still be watching the house.

When the scene had finally been cleared at two this morning, he'd stationed Deputy McKinley at the house until his shift was over at seven. That left an hour and forty-five minutes for the perp to have deposited the box without witnesses. Cody's stomach churned at the thought of what could have happened to Maggie.

Even more important than when the person left the box was how had he gotten the rings in the first place? Had he been in the house before Maggie returned to Whitehaven, or had he been able to sneak in sometime during the night?

He took a side-glance at Maggie. Her eyes were closed as she leaned against the cabinet and the fingers of her right hand clung to the cross hanging from her neck. He considered walking over to comfort her, but the thought of her recoiling from his hand stopped him.

Standing in her drive that evening, lying to her, telling her she didn't mean anything to him had almost ripped his heart from his chest. He'd always imagined that, though the pain he had inflicted upon on himself had lingered, she would have moved past the hurt to a happier and healthier life. Based on her behavior now though, he realized he was probably wrong. How many times had she clung to that cross in the days after he'd let her go?

He shook his head to clear his thoughts.

Revisiting their past wouldn't help the current situation. He needed to focus on how the perp had gotten into the house. The night before, he had personally walked the outside perimeter of the house and hadn't seen any broken windows or doors. Deputy McKinley had checked the interior and hadn't reported anything amiss.

"Maggie, how do you think someone got into the house? Were any of the doors or windows broken when you arrived?"

She didn't move, just continued sitting there, clinging to the cross. He was about to ask again when she opened her eyes. "No, nothing was open or broken. Jacob said he made sure the house was locked up tight after the funeral."

If all the doors had been locked and there weren't any broken windows, the perp was either an expert lock picker or had a key. He couldn't imagine Mr. Jones or Jake giving a key to anyone.

"Does anyone else have a key to the house? Could your dad have given one to someone and not tell you?"

Maggie stood there thinking, her auburn hair cascading over her shoulders.

"I suppose he could have, but surely he would have told me." Her eyes widened in surprise, like she thought of something. "Remember when we were kids? We always had a spare key hidden

28

in a toolbox in the garage. Mom was always afraid she would lock herself out."

How could he forget about that key? The Joneses had gone out of town on a vacation one summer and had asked Cody to house sit. After locking himself out, he'd had to call them. Mrs. Jones had laughed and told him about the key. She'd said she'd had to use it a couple times.

"I'm going to go check and see if it's still there. In case it is, can you find me a sandwich bag to put the key in? It's a long shot, but if the perp used it maybe he left his prints."

Sandwich bag in hand, he walked to the garage. The tools and boxes in the garage were covered with a thick layer of dust. All but one toolbox. The one that held the spare key had four perfectly clean stripes on the lid. A perfect fit for fingers. Pulling his multipurpose tool from his pocket, he used the corkscrew to pick up the key through the key hole. He placed it in the bag and sealed it before returning to Maggie in the kitchen.

He waved the bag as he walked in. "That's it. That's how our guy got in. Everything in the garage was covered in dust, but someone had been in the toolbox recently." Placing the key on the counter next to the box, Cody faced Maggie. "I need to take the toolbox, key, and rings in for processing. I'd really like for you to find somewhere else to stay until we can find the guy who is doing this."

"Cody, I have nothing. My mother is gone, my father is gone, and Jacob is God knows where. All I have left of the people I love is this house. The house is going on the market soon and these are probably the last few weeks I will ever have here." Her voice cracked on the last sentence. "I will not let anyone take that from me. Gary called this morning and said my exterior paint is in. I'll go into town and talk to him about a home security system and new locks, too."

She pulled a trash bag from the supply closet, handed it to him, and nodded toward the evidence sitting on the counter. She picked up her list of supplies, grabbed her purse from the counter, and walked out of the kitchen. Still wearing the latex gloves, Cody placed the box and the key in the trash bag. He'd have to let forensics know that Maggie and Amelia had handled the box. He followed Maggie out.

All I have left of the people I love is this house. He wanted to tell her he was still here. She had loved him once, even though he hadn't thought he was worthy of her love. On that warm summer night, he had known she deserved a man a hundred times better than he was, and he had let her go.

FIVE

The trip into town didn't seem to take as long as normal. Of course, she had spent the entire ride thinking about the package that had been on the doorstep that morning. She didn't know who had sent it or why. *No, they didn't just send it; they delivered it in person.* Someone had been at the house, on the porch, while she was sleeping. Fear and anger fought for dominance within her.

Not only had they been at the house to deliver the package but, at some point, they had been *in* the house. They had gone through her parents' things and had taken two of the most precious items she had left of them.

She pulled into the hardware store's parking lot. Gary was at the customer service desk when she walked in. "Hey, Gary. How are you this morning?"

"I'm doing well, Ms. Maggie. Did you get that list of those supplies you need?"

"I do have my list, but I want to ask you about new locks and a home security system. I've had a little trouble at the house, and I think it's time I changed the locks and set up a security system." Maggie laid her purse on the counter and started digging for her supply list.

"I'm sorry to hear that. A nice girl like you shouldn't be out there all alone. Why, you should have a man to take care of you. But that's none of my business.

"Gary. It's the twenty-first century. I'm quite capable of taking care of myself."

"You're right. Just ignore me. We do have some basic security items, door and window alarms that would probably do for a house here in town. But if I were you, I'd consider calling the security company in Prairie's Grove. With your house so far out, you'd want something that can cover the perimeter and call for help if it were to ever go off." He led her toward the aisle with the alarms.

She listened to him describe each product and chose an alarm for the front and back doors of the house and alarms for all the downstairs windows. She also grabbed some motion sensor lights for the front and back porches as well. She followed Gary around the store as he helped her gather the remaining items on her list.

"Let me get that business card for you, and then I'll help you out to your car." Gary dug around the service desk.

"Thank you, but I can manage to carry everything out."

"Nonsense. I want to help." He lifted the phone and looked under it before setting it back down. "Besides, they keep this place too cold. I need to warm up a bit, thin skin and all." She chuckled. It was close to one hundred degrees outside. It was hard to imagine how anyone could be cold.

He shuffled through various baskets and drawers. "Here it is." He handed over a small, white business card. She stuffed it in her wallet, making a mental note to call them when she returned to the house.

He grabbed her bags and waited for her to lead the way to the truck.

After Gary placed the painting supplies and security stuff in the bed of the truck, she gave him a wave and thanked him for his help.

The next stop was the grocery store to stock the cabinets. The parking lot was full. It seemed as if everyone else in town had run out of food at the same time. Parking at the end of the lot by the side alley, she hoped her previous purchases would be okay in the bed of the truck.

Once inside the store, she grabbed a shopping cart and headed to the fruits and vegetables. With the events of the past twenty-four hours, she could use some comfort food. She picked up a couple bunches of bananas so she could make her mother's banana pudding for dessert. She also picked up some fresh tomatoes and lettuce.

Slowly making her way across the grocery store, Maggie picked up enough food for a couple of weeks. She wanted to stay out of town as much as possible. Running into Cody at the sheriff's station yesterday and then having him at her house twice in the last twelve hours had added to the ache in her chest. If she didn't have to come to town she wouldn't take the chance of running into him.

He had hurt her so deeply. He'd told her he loved her and then had taken it all back before completely cutting her out of his life. What had been wrong with her? She thought she'd been a good girlfriend. She had replayed every conversation they'd had in the days preceding that night and couldn't think of anything. She hadn't been clingy. He'd told her many times how beautiful she was, inside and out.

After he broke things off, he wouldn't take her calls or return her messages. Wanting an explanation, she had called him twice. After that, she'd refused to play the desperate girlfriend calling him multiple times. She'd never understood his change of heart but had worked hard to stop thinking about it. Those old wounds were not going to be opened now.

Groceries paid for, she wheeled them to the truck. She hadn't realized how long she'd spent in the grocery store, but it must have been a while because the parking lot was nearly deserted now. As she got closer to the truck, a folded piece of paper under the windshield caught her eye. Probably a flier from one of the local churches inviting her to church or an advertisement. She loaded the groceries into the bed of the truck, taking note that all her bags from the hardware store were still accounted for.

She grabbed the paper off the windshield, put it in the passenger seat, and climbed into the truck. Sticking the key in the ignition and turning, the truck sputtered and died. This couldn't be happening right now. It couldn't break down now, not when she had frozen goods that needed to be put in the freezer. She tried the key again, and the truck sputtered dismally but finally turned over. Thankful that potential disaster had been averted, she reached over and picked up the paper that had been tucked under her windshield wiper.

The words "I'm watching you" were spelled out using magazine clippings. Her hands shook, and she whipped her head up, surveying the parking lot. When she didn't see anyone, she looked at the flier again. "Join us as Whitehaven High School's Drama Club presents Mystery Dinner Theatre 'Stalked.'" The fear that had been vibrating up and down her spine whooshed away. It was a flier. There was nothing to be afraid of. She was just jumpy from the last twenty-four hours. She wadded up the paper and threw it in the passenger's side floorboard. As she turned to grab her seat belt, a face appeared in the window.

She let out a squeal at Cody's face staring back at her. She cranked the window down. "Cody, what are you doing, besides giving me a heart attack?"

"I saw the truck in the parking lot and wanted to check on you." He was so handsome standing there, blue eyes sparkling in the sunlight. His blond hair was slightly longer than he had kept it years ago. She wanted to reach up and run her fingers through it but kept her hands clasped in her lap.

"I'm fine." She willed her heart to slow.

"That's good. I got the evidence turned in. They're going to dust them for fingerprints." He rested his arms on the truck door.

34

"Will I get the rings back?" Those were the only two things of her parent's that she wanted. It symbolized so much of them and their relationship. Those rings stood for what she wanted in her own marriage.

"It may take a couple of days, but I promise you will get them back. You probably don't want to hear this, but I still think you should stay somewhere else tonight."

"You're right. I don't want to hear that. Thank you for the concern. I bought new locks and some alarms for the doors and windows. I even got motion lights. I'm going to call a security company about having a system installed. Now if you'll excuse me, I have some frozen food that I need to get home." A look she couldn't interpret crossed his face, but he stepped back without a word. She put the truck in gear and drove out of the parking lot.

She risked a glance in the rearview mirror. Cody stood rooted in spot, watching her drive away. Her heart clenched a bit. This is what it was like to drive away from someone she loved. And she had loved him once, and maybe she still had those feelings buried deep. She wasn't sure Cody had really loved her, though.

She had to make several trips to get everything into the house. As she was grabbing the last bag, tires on gravel alerted her to the arrival of a vehicle. A Dale County Sheriff's cruiser pulled in. Her heart fluttered momentarily. Had Cody chased after her? Had she wanted him to?

It only lasted a moment before she reminded herself Cody didn't want her, and she didn't need him. She needed to get the house sold and get back to Houston.

The car stopped, and Deputy Grainger stepped out. "Good afternoon, Ms. Jones. I'm Deputy Michael Grainger, but you can call me Grainger."

"Good afternoon. Please call me Maggie."

"Yes, ma'am. I was pulling in to check on the property. Any problems?"

"Not that I've noticed. I just got back from town."

"Would it be okay if I looked around? Just to make sure?"

"No problem. Come on in when you're done, and I'll get you a glass of tea."

"Thank you."

She carried the bags to the kitchen and started putting the groceries away until she found the jug of tea she'd purchased.

"Ma'am?" Grainger's voice came from the doorway. "I've looked around outside. Mind if I come inside? You said you were gone for a spell."

"Do you think it's necessary?" Maybe Cody was right. Maybe she should find somewhere else to stay.

"No, ma'am. I don't, but it might make you feel better."

"It's Maggie. I don't see the harm in it. Go ahead. I'll have your tea ready when you're done."

He nodded and disappeared down the hall. She filled a cup with ice and poured the tea before finishing putting the groceries up. She was laying the alarms and new locks on the island when Grainger returned.

"Just as I thought it would be, everything is fine. Would you like some help with those?" He nodded to the items on the island.

She handed him the glass of tea. "No. Thank you. I think I can manage."

"Okay then. I'm going to head back out on patrol. One of us will pull up occasionally. We won't get out unless we see something suspicious or you call in and ask us. I just started my shift, so it'll be me the next twelve hours. Why don't I give you my cell number?"

"That would be great." The fear she'd had when he'd asked to look around had started to dissipate. Having his number helped. This way, if something else were to happen, she could call for help but still bypass Cody completely.

She pulled her phone out of her pocket and typed his number into her contacts. Then she sent him a text. His phone beeped from his pocket. "Now you'll have my number."

He smiled and drained his glass. "Thanks again for the tea. I'll see myself out. Call or text if you need anything."

"I will." She gave him a little wave and went back to the alarms and locks on display. She was going to start by changing the lock and alarming the front door. She grabbed the boxes and tools she needed and set to work.

SIX

Cody stirred the vegetables on the stovetop as his thoughts bounced back and forth between Iris's case and Maggie's. In both situations the stalker used notes, but Maggie's stalker started off with threats whereas Iris's had almost seemed like a secret admirer. He didn't know if they were related or not. If they were, he'd have to consider pulling Grainger off the case. He was one of the department's best deputies, but his sister's case and subsequent death were fresh for the department and even more so for Grainger.

Then there was Maggie. She'd seemed more receptive to him at the grocery store. Her words had remained just as distant, but something in her expression had softened when she'd first recognized him. He knew it had only been a couple hours since he'd seen her, but it didn't stop him from wanting to see her again.

Now she was alone out there at the Jones' house. Maybe he should call to check on her. He doubted she would stay on the phone long. He could drive over there, but what would he say? *I was just in the neighborhood... twenty minutes outside of town.* That would probably go over about as well as a phone call, but he had to know she was okay. If he could get her on the phone for a few minutes and hear her voice, he could ease his worry.

He stirred the vegetables once more and dug his cell phone out of his pocket. He dialed the home number and waited while it rang. Five rings and it went to the answering machine.

"Maggie, this is—"

"Hello, are you there? I'm here. Sorry, I left the phone in another room." She panted, like she'd been running.

"I was calling to check on you."

"Thank you, Sheriff. I'm fine at this moment. I got the locks changed and all of the alarms installed."

He was glad to hear that she was taking steps to protect herself, even if they weren't the steps he wanted her to take.

"The security company will be coming to set up a more sophisticated system in a couple of days. I've also noticed a cruiser pull up into the drive occasionally. I met Deputy Grainger when he came to check on me. Thank you for that." Her breathing slowed to normal. She was cordial, but it was still obvious that she hadn't been kidding when she told him that he was the Sheriff and she would be treating him as such.

"That's good. Deputy Grainger is one of my best deputies." Knowing that Grainger had made contact with her and was taking his job seriously helped ease the worry.

"Did you need anything else?"

"Magpie, don't do this."

"Don't call me Magpie. And *This*? *This* is something you created six years ago. *This* is your fault. *This* is me protecting my already shattered heart. You said you loved me. You were the silver lining in the dark clouds that invaded my life that summer. Then out of nowhere you ended it. So, no, I don't want to talk to you. Now, if you have no official business, I'm going to hang up. I have lots of work to do." Her voice quaked as she spoke.

Her words weren't angry, but full of hurt, and it tore at his heart.

"I'm sorry Maggie. I didn't mean to hurt you like that. It—"

"Business?"

"Okay. We checked the beanbag, toolbox, key, and box for fingerprints. There weren't any. A deputy will continue to check your property occasionally. If anything weird happens, or if you need someone, please call it in, okay?"

"Thank you. I will call if I need anything. Goodnight."

With that, she hung up. He stood there staring at the screen of his cell phone. He'd really messed things up back then. He had loved her, but after the conversation with Jake that night, he knew he would be holding her back.

BEEP. BEEP. BEEP. The fire alarm went off. He hadn't stirred the vegetables and now they were burning in the pan. It was just as well. The hurt in her voice had chased away his appetite. He turned the burner off and set the pan on the stovetop.

Some day he would sit Maggie down and explain to her. It wouldn't be anytime soon, though. He needed to keep his full attention on the present situation.

He went to his home office and grabbed the laptop. Taking it to the kitchen, he turned it on and let it boot up while he made himself a glass of iced tea. He needed to figure out who was terrorizing Maggie. Someone obviously wanted to scare her away, but why? Maggie hadn't seemed to think that the motivation was a personal vendetta. From her account, she lived a quiet life. Maybe it had something to do with her father's property. Mr. Jones had owned several hundred acres on the outskirts of town near the border to Mexico. Cody supposed that terrorizing Maggie could possibly make her want to stay away from the area, or even convince Jake that they should sell the land.

He dismissed that idea as quickly as it had come to him. Mr. Jones hadn't reported any problems to him or Maggie for that matter. The smashed mailbox and vandalized house didn't necessarily mean anything, but coupled with the message on the answering machine and the rings, it pointed to someone with a personal grudge against Maggie. It was more like Iris's case.

Whitehaven was a quiet town. It had its share of drunks, juvenile delinquents, and vandals but no serious criminals. Iris's case was the most serious one they'd had in Whitehaven in as long as he could remember. He had been a deputy with the Sheriff's department for four years prior to being elected Sheriff. Not only had Iris been Grainger's sister, but she'd been an emergency dispatcher, so Cody had been fairly well acquainted with her. It had made her case all the more upsetting.

Her stalker had started with seemingly nonthreatening gifts. She had received several anonymous flower deliveries and candies. She had chalked it up to either a secret admirer or the family member of someone she had helped when they'd called 911. But the gifts had turned more sinister—black roses and even a dead rat. Not long after that, she'd been physically attacked.

Were they dealing with a serial stalker? If so, he couldn't limit his search to Whitehaven and Dale County. He'd have to expand his search parameters. He pulled up his email to instruct Deputy Grainger to start searching for any similar incidents in the surrounding counties and possibly branch out to the whole state.

The notes Maggie received had a familiar ring to them. After sending the email, he pulled up the internet browser and typed in "one for sorrow." There was a plethora of results ranging from music to books, but an old nursery rhyme caught his eye. It not only contained "one for sorrow" but also "two for joy." That's why it was so familiar, he had probably heard some version of the rhyme growing up.

How could this be connected to Maggie? He clicked a link, and his pulse kicked up a notch. The nursery rhyme was about the Magpie bird. *Magpie.* It was no secret that he and Jake called Maggie Magpie. No one else ever called her that. This was definitely personal.

He pulled out his cell phone and dialed Jake's cell number. It was a long shot that Jake would even have his personal cell phone with him. The call went straight to voicemail.

"Jake. This is Cody. Give me a call as soon as you can." He would try the security company Jake worked for in the morning.

Knowing Maggie wasn't just a victim picked at random, Cody felt compelled to make sure she was safe. She didn't answer the home phone and when he tried her cell phone, it went straight to voicemail. Unease crept up. He couldn't sit and do nothing. He closed the laptop, grabbed his keys, and locked up the house. He was going to go see Maggie. Perhaps with this new information, she'd consider finding another place to stay.

SEVEN

She'd spent the afternoon changing the locks and installing the alarms on all the windows and doors. After managing to get some cleaning and sorting done in her bedroom, her stomach growled. It was a good time for a break. She placed a frozen dinner in the microwave and went to get the newest novel she'd been reading. Reading about lost love and eating the banana pudding that was setting in the refrigerator would be a good way to finish the evening.

She sighed deeply. Being here dredged up all the old feelings of pain and rejection, surprisingly strong and fresh in her heart. She had loved once, then he was gone, and he'd taken her heart with him. After that, she'd never gone looking for love again. The rejection was just too painful to go through again. Cody had deemed her unworthy. There had been some flaw that she hadn't seen, nor had she been able to find. So now, she found love in her books and poured herself into her job, tutoring children, and writing when her schedule would allow.

The microwave beeped. She grabbed the cardboard container, a fork, and a bottle of water from the refrigerator and went to make herself comfortable on the old, worn out couch in the living room.

Her cell phone flashed a notification light. She had missed a call. She swiped the screen and saw that the call had been from Cody. He was probably calling to check on her. She'd call him back after she ate.

No sooner had she opened her book and put the first bite of noodles in her mouth, there was a knock on the door. She found herself wishing she hadn't put her father's gun away. Who was she kidding? Bad guys didn't typically knock, right? She stood to answer the door and there was another knock, followed by the unmistakable baritone voice of the sheriff himself.

"Magpie? I know you're in there. I can smell burnt cardboard. You're sitting on the couch, reading a book, aren't you?"

She settled herself back down on to the couch and forked in another mouthful of noodles. She was predictable. He knew it. She knew it. So, what? "What do you want?" she yelled around the food in her mouth.

"You didn't answer the phone."

"Sorry. I was cleaning upstairs."

"Can I come in?" His question was slightly muffled by the big wooden door.

"No!" She reached for her book and flipped to the page that was marked with her favorite bookmark.

"Come on, Maggie. I want to talk."

He wants to talk. What can he possibly want to talk about? She couldn't stand the thought of listening to whatever he had to say.

"So, talk," she said in the direction of the door.

"I am not going to talk to you through the door."

"Well, I'm not letting you in, so we are at an impasse."

"You have always been so stubborn." His heavy footsteps descended the porch.

Finally. She smirked in victory, stuffed another bite into her mouth, and got lost in her book. A few minutes passed and movement across the room startled her. Gasping, she stood, knocking everything to the floor. Cody stepped into the room, cocking an eyebrow at the mess.

"What in the world are you doing?" she yelled at him while picking up the closest thing she could find to throw at him.

He smiled and caught the pillow before it could hit him in the face. "I came to check on you." He threw the pillow back at her.

She knocked the pillow to the floor and stared at him. If looks could kill, he'd be a dead man.

"So, you decided that since I wouldn't let you in you would break in? Newsflash, *Sheriff*, that is illegal."

"I wouldn't classify it as breaking in really. I just used an alternative entrance." He chuckled at his own joke.

Her heart rate was finally slowing to normal.

"What alternative entrance? Did you bring the spare key back with you?"

"Nope. The same one Jake and I used to sneak in and out of the house."

She'd forgotten he had spent so much time at the house and knew all the nooks and crannies just like she and Jacob did. Apparently, he'd climbed the old tree and jiggled Jacob's bedroom window until the lock flew open. She made a mental note to put something above the window to keep it from opening until the security company came.

She bent down and cleaned up the noodles that had spilled onto the floor. She set the bowl on the coffee table and sat on the sofa.

"You ruined my meal, so thanks for that," she grumbled.

"I am sorry I startled you. But we do need to talk. It's important."

"I guess you're not going to leave until you say whatever it is you came to say." She gestured for him to take the chair diagonal to the couch. Cody sat and turned to her.

"I did a quick internet search on the phrases from the two notes you received. *One for sorrow* and *two for joy*. Those are lines from an old nursery rhyme."

She'd thought she had heard them before but hadn't been able to place the origin.

"There are several different versions of the rhyme, anywhere from six to fourteen lines long. It's in reference to a bird, and the superstitions connected to the amount of birds one sees."

"Okay. What does a bird or group of birds have to do with me?"

"Maggie, it's not just any bird. It's the Magpie bird."

She felt sick. Only Jacob and Cody had ever called her that. The situation no longer seemed like just a frightening prank, but a deeply personal violation of her life. Cody leaned forward to rest his forearms on his knees, an earnest expression on his face. She had a hard time focusing on him.

"I believe whoever is behind this is targeting you specifically, and that they won't stop until the rhyme is finished."

The room started to spin, and she couldn't breathe. Loud pounding filled her ears, and her lungs ached for air. Her vision started to go black, and then she was pushed forward until her head was between her knees. A warm hand rubbed her back. The pounding faded, and she could hear Cody speaking comforting words to her.

The warmth of his hand spread through her entire being. She focused on that warmth and slowly her composure returned. Focusing on her breathing, she sat up and looked at Cody. His eyes were filled with concern. He took both her hands in his and rubbed the back of her hand with his thumb, the comforting gesture he had done whenever she'd had moments of grief after her mother's death.

She had missed him so much, but she couldn't sit here and allow herself to open back up to him. She pulled her hands from his and stood to put some distance between them.

"Why would someone be targeting me? Like I told you before, nothing in my life justifies this kind of craziness." She paced in front of the coffee table.

"I'm just as confused as you are. But apparently, this *is* about you." He stood and placed his hands on her shoulders, stopping her pacing. "With this new information, it's best if you find a more secure place to stay."

She shrugged his hands from her shoulders. "I've already told you. I am not going to be bullied into leaving. I've taken every available precaution to keep myself safe. I've got new locks, window and door alarms."

"Maggie, you need to take this seriously. I was able to get in through Jake's window without you knowing. The house isn't as secure as you think."

"That's true, but you were here more than you were at your own house. You know all the secrets of this old house."

He cupped her cheek in his hand. "I care about you. I couldn't stand it if anything happened to you."

She cringed at his words, at his touch, and turned her head, breaking contact. She was silent for a moment. Was he telling the truth? Did he care for her as his Magpie or as a case? She took a step back and turned her head. "Why would I believe you?" The truth was she didn't know what to believe anymore.

"Maggie, please let me explain." He pleaded with his eyes. The anguish she saw in them only intensified her own.

"I'd rather not." She didn't want to hear about why he'd rejected her. What about her had turned him away. She picked up her mess from the coffee table and disappeared into the kitchen.

She threw away the trash and crossed to the sink. Tears slowly streamed down her cheeks. His eyes told her everything she needed to know. He was truly sorry for what he had done, and he wanted her to know why he had made his decision. She wasn't ready to hear it. She wasn't ready to finally know what was wrong with her.

She turned on the cold water and splashed her face. Her eyes cooled, she dried her face. She grabbed two bottles of water and went back to face Cody.

She handed him a bottle and took her seat on the couch. "You said that this nursery rhyme had several lines. The first line was 'One for sorrow.' I assume that was why there was only one shot? And 'Two for joy' would be the rings because two people get married and that is a joyous occasion. What's the next line?"

"In most versions, it's 'three for a girl' and then 'four for a boy'. I really don't know what to think about those."

She remembered a baby shower she went to recently. "You know, there are old wives' tales about predicting the sex of babies. Maybe that is what those two lines refer to. I'm not pregnant and in no position to be so anytime soon, so I don't think whoever is doing this will interpret it that way."

Cody's shoulders seemed to relax when she mentioned she was unattached, or had it been a figment of her imagination? Was he hoping to rekindle their relationship? That wasn't going to happen.

"I hate sitting here wondering when and if someone will strike next." She yawned, exhausted from the stress.

"Maggie, please reconsider what I said about staying somewhere else. I know you don't want to be bullied, but I'm talking about your safety."

"I'm not leaving. Like I said before, the locks are changed, the door and windows are alarmed, and you've got a deputy checking on me. I also have dad's old pistol, if it becomes necessary."

He looked her in the eye. "Call me if you need anything, even if you think it's silly. There is nothing silly about your safety."

She nodded.

"I'll go so you can get some rest." He stood and walked to the door. "I'll use the front door this time. I did place an old metal bar I found in Jake's room above the window to keep it from opening."

"Thank you." She followed behind him and disabled the alarm on the door.

"Lock the door and set the alarm behind me. And, please, call if you need something. Anything."

She closed the door and set the alarm.

Before heading to bed, she paused at the bedroom window. Could someone be out there watching her? Maybe she should have listened to Cody. She raised the blinds, illuminating the drive below.

Cody's car was still parked outside. He looked up. Her heart fluttered at the sight of him standing guard. Despite the anger she harbored, she was grateful he cared enough to stay. She shook her head and gave him a small wave before closing the blinds and getting ready for bed.

EIGHT

Sunlight streaming through the window woke Maggie. She checked the drive first thing. Cody's car was gone. He must have left when dawn broke or perhaps he'd been called away on an emergency.

His face last night, when he'd practically begged to explain himself, had been compelling. Maybe she should hear him out. The only thing stopping her from hearing his side was she was afraid of what he was going to say. Amelia had given her the impression Cody had acted like he'd been the one whose heart had been broken and not the one breaking hearts. She wasn't ready to find out what she had been lacking back then.

She pushed away from the window and started getting ready for her breakfast with Cassie, her best friend from high school. She'd called the day before Maggie had arrived in Whitehaven and asked Maggie to have breakfast with her at the old diner in town. It was a welcome relief. Maggie definitely needed a distraction.

She locked up the house and climbed into the old truck. Just like it had been since she got to town, it was stubborn and didn't want to start. She turned the key again, gave it some gas, and the engine roared to life. She tuned the radio to the local Christian station and headed into town.

When she arrived at the diner, Cassie was sitting in a booth at the rear of the restaurant. When Cassie saw her, her eyes lit up. She stepped from the booth and gave Maggie a huge hug. They slid into the booth as the waitress came to take their order.

"Good morning, ladies. What can I get you to drink?"

"I'll take a glass of orange juice." Maggie smiled. The waitress was young, probably still in high school. Her blond hair hung down to her shoulders, the tips a light shade of purple. "I love your hair."

"Thanks. My sister is in beauty school so guess who gets to be the guinea pig?"

"I think it looks great," Cassie chimed from across the table.

The waitress blushed at the compliments.

"Thank you. I've got an orange juice for you, and what can I get for you?" The waitress turned to Cassie.

"I'll take water with lemon."

"Great. Are you ready to order, or do you need more time?"

"I'm ready if you are." Cassie looked to Maggie.

Maggie looked over the menu quickly, searching for her favorite breakfast food. She found it. "I'm ready, too. I'll have the French toast platter with extra bacon."

The waitress jotted down the order. "And for you?"

"I'll have the same." Cassie handed her their menus. "Thank you."

"I'll go put your order in and be right back with your drinks." The girl disappeared into the kitchen.

"So, Maggie, how's it going?" Cassie asked after the waitress left.

She told her about the vandalism, leaving out the beanbag attack, and the stolen rings. She didn't want to worry her friend.

"I can't believe anyone would do that. Do you think there's more vandalism you haven't seen yet?"

"No. I walked around the house and looked before I went to the sheriff's station."

"So, you know Cody Smith is the new sheriff, then."

"Unfortunately, I do."

The waitress dropped off their drinks and bustled away.

"I take it that means you've already seen him?" Cassie pulled the lemon off the rim of the glass and squeezed the juice into her water before dropping the whole slice in.

"I have. A couple of times."

"Are you okay with that?" Cassie took a drink.

"Not really. He wants to talk about things. I don't. I don't want to know what was wrong with me that drove him away." She wadded up the straw wrapper.

"I'm going to tell you now, like I told you then, he's an idiot. That's what was wrong."

"I'd like to believe that." She gave a half-hearted smile. "How are things on the baby front?" Maggie knew Cassie and Hank were trying for a baby. Maggie hoped the change of subject would take her friend's attention away from her and Cody.

"I'm not pregnant yet, but we're still trying. We haven't given up. It's all in God's timing. How about you? Any big plans for your birthday? Two more days and you'll be a quarter of a century."

Maggie had hoped no one would remember. This was a year she didn't feel like celebrating. "No plans. I'm not really in a mood for celebrating. You know what I mean?"

"I can only imagine how you feel. I won't press you into doing anything, but I do think you should get out of that house on your birthday. If you feel up to it, I'll treat you to a birthday lunch."

"Thanks. I'll think about it."

"How's your writing? I keep waiting on an email saying you've gotten a contract." Cassie wiggled her eyebrows.

"It's not." Another thing she was no good at.

"Oh, no. Which publishers have you tried?" Growing up, Maggie had told her how much she'd dreamed of a full-time writing career. In high school, Cassie would talk about graduating high school, marrying her boyfriend, and starting a family. Maggie would dream along with her, except hers would be a world full of stories and books. At one time, she'd pictured Cody by her side during all of it.

"Just that first one I told you about. They sent back a long list of why they didn't want it." She'd cried after getting that email. There was so much wrong with the manuscript. She thought she would be able to fix it and resubmit, but every time she opened the document, she was reminded of what a failure she was.

"You should try some more. It might not have fit with that publisher, but that doesn't mean there's not one out there that will love it. Don't give up." Cassie had always been her personal cheerleader. Always encouraging her.

"Oh, I'm not... I've just been so busy during the school year and, well, I'm here this summer."

Cassie's face fell. "I know. Do you need help at your dad's place? I could come help."

"No. I can manage. There's just so much to go through. I can't decide what to keep and what to get rid of." She wanted to keep it all. Sorting and getting rid of his stuff was so final.

The waitress came to the table and placed their food in front of them. "Bon appétit."

"Thank you so much." Maggie smiled at the waitress.

Their breakfast was enjoyable. Her food was mouth-watering, and the reprieve from her constant worries over the house and the threats was a much-needed break. After Maggie paid for breakfast, she gave Cassie a hug good-bye at the door, and they parted ways. Maggie's hand had barely grabbed the door handle of the truck when a scream let out from across the parking lot.

The only other person that she remembered seeing in the parking lot was Cassie, and Maggie took off at a run in her direction. Cassie was standing next to her vehicle with her hand over her mouth. Maggie came to an abrupt halt next to her. Cassie's normally pristine car was covered in red paint. The same shade that adorned the side of Maggie's house. There was a message wiped in the paint on the windshield, *Three for a girl.*

With sweaty palms, Maggie pulled her phone from her pocket and dialed the sheriff's office. She and Cassie decided to wait on the bench outside the diner. Cody was the first law enforcement officer to arrive, parking his cruiser in front of them.

He climbed from the cruiser and walked to them. His crisp Dale County Sheriff's shirt was pulled taut over his torso, and his utility belt rested perfectly on his hips. He was the picture of strength. It took all she had not to run to him, throw herself into his arms, and let him be her protector.

"Hey. What happened?" He looked from her to Cassie and then back to her.

She slowly shook her head. "Someone vandalized Cassie's car."

"Did you see anyone around the car? Cassie, do you know anyone that would want to do that?"

"It's not just vandalism to Cassie's car." Maggie stood with shaky legs. "It's the third line."

Cody's eyes widened in alarm. "Where's the car?"

She nodded toward the parking lot. "I'll show you."

Cody and Cassie followed her. After a few feet, the car came into view. There was so much red paint, she couldn't tell what color the car was supposed to be. The red liquid dripped onto the concrete, creating large pools under the car.

She stopped, as did Cassie. They didn't want to go any further. Her stomach churned at the sight in front of her.

Cody let out a heavy sigh before taking his radio from its clip on his shoulder. "Dee, call the Whitehaven police department, and have them send an officer to Earl's Diner. Tell them they're gonna need a tow truck and tarps. If Deputy Grainger is free, send him, too." He clipped the radio back in its place and pulled his phone from his pocket. He circled the car taking pictures from several angles. "On top of the paint and the message, the tires have been slashed."

After he took a few more pictures, they all walked back to the bench where she and Cassie took their seats. "Unfortunately, this happened in the city, so it's not my jurisdiction. Dee's going to send Whitehaven PD. They're gonna want to ask you some questions, and they won't be able to release the car to you, Cassie. Do you have someone who can pick you up, or do I need to arrange for a deputy to take you home?"

Cassie started to speak, but Maggie interrupted her, guilt inching its way in her conscience. "It's my fault that this has happened. I'll take her home, and then we can call about getting her a rental car."

"No, it absolutely is *not* your fault. Don't even think that." Cody's face was severe.

Cassie nodded. "He's right. Some psycho trashing my car has nothing to do with you. I'll take that ride when Sheriff Smith says it's okay to leave though. Thank you, Maggie. I just wish I knew what was going on."

She grabbed Cassie's hand, trying to decide how to tell her best friend that her being targeted by a criminal had caused this.

"Remember when I told you that some trouble had happened since I got to town? Well, it's actually a little more than vandalism. Someone took a shot at me the first night I was here. Whoever it was, broke in the house, stole my parents' wedding rings, and had them delivered back to me at the house. And now your car. I didn't want to worry you, but it appears my stalker has decided to bring you into it."

Cassie's mouth formed a perfect *O* before she placed her hand over it.

"I'm so sorry, Cassie."

"Maggie, please don't blame yourself," Cody repeated. "This is not your fault."

Cassie squeezed Maggie's hand. "Cody is absolutely right. But I don't understand why whoever it was would vandalize my car to get at you."

"He's using lines from an old nursery rhyme every time he threatens me. *Three for a girl* was wiped in the paint on your car. I guess he decided to take advantage of our breakfast." Maggie stared off into the distance, trying to understand what was going on. Cody had said the next line after three would be "Four for a boy." Would that mean an act of terror would be inflicted on a male close to her?

She knew Jacob was out of town on work, so she didn't think it could be aimed at him. The only other male she was even remotely close to was Cody. She inhaled suddenly and glanced at him.

"What is it Maggie?" He had been watching her the whole time.

"Um, I guess it's leftover adrenaline from all of this." She would talk with him later.

A Whitehaven police cruiser, followed by another Dale County Sheriff's vehicle, pulled up behind Cody's cruiser. She recognized Deputy Grainger as he stepped from the Dale County cruiser.

Cody met the officers out of earshot. She couldn't hear what they were saying as she sat there, taking in his six-foot frame. He'd added another couple inches and some bulk to that frame since the time they'd been together. She thought it suited him well.

She was still staring when Cody turned and looked straight at her. He smiled a knowing smile. She abruptly looked away, feeling her face flush at being caught gawking at him. Cody would be able to tell she was embarrassed; her pale skin had always betrayed her.

She turned to Cassie. "I'm so sorry for this. I had no idea this would happen, or I would have canceled our breakfast." Tears pooled in her eyes.

"Maggie, don't you dare apologize. You are not at fault. It's only a car. Hank hated that thing anyway. He'll be happy it's gone for a while. I'll call my insurance company and get everything taken care of." Cassie wrapped her arms around Maggie and squeezed so tight, Maggie was afraid she'd pass out.

"Maggie. Cassie. I think you two can go for now." Cody strode back up to their bench. "I'm going to stay here. If we need anything else, I'll call. Maggie, where will I be able to find you later? I really don't think you should be home alone."

Maggie didn't want to go home alone either, but she wasn't going to let Cody know she needed him. She was about to make something up when Cassie spoke. "Maggie will be at my house the rest of the day."

"Cassie, I don't know if I should. I mean, I've already caused you trouble. What if my being at your house brings this person to you?"

"Nonsense. I won't take no for an answer. Besides, it's Hank's seventy-two hour off shift. Unless there is some kind of fiery catastrophe, he'll be home." Cassie squeezed Maggie's hand.

"Good. I'll see you at Cassie's when we're done wrapping things up here." Cody nodded before turning his attention to a third cruiser pulling up to the diner.

Cassie made idle chitchat as Maggie drove them straight to Cassie's house. She knew Cassie was trying to keep her mind occupied by telling her about her new decorating business. Two years ago, Cassie's parents had moved to Florida and sold their house to her and Hank. When they'd arrived at the house, she insisted that Maggie take a look around and see all the work she'd done. She'd chatted cheerfully throughout the tour.

They had barely sat down with their sodas at Cassie's kitchen table when someone rang the doorbell. "Hank's in the living room, he'll get it," Cassie assured her.

Maggie heard Cody's unmistakable voice drift in from the living room. Moments later, his figure filled the doorway.

"Cassie. Maggie." He nodded at each of them. "Cassie, I filled Hank in on the status of your car. The incident report should be

60

ready tomorrow afternoon and then you can turn it over to your insurance company."

He turned his attention in Maggie's direction, and she could feel the butterflies start making waves in her stomach. How could he still affect her this way?

"Maggie, if you're ready, I have some questions."

Maggie nodded. She stood, put her cup in the sink, and gave Cassie a hug. She said good-bye to Hank and followed Cody out of the house and down the drive to where their vehicles were parked. Maggie was looking down, watching where she was walking and thinking about the events that had filled the last couple days, when she ran into something hard. She looked up into Cody's handsome face, not realizing he had stopped to turn around.

He reached up and placed his hands on her upper arms to steady her. The heat from his touch radiated straight to her stomach and brought the butterflies from earlier to full flutter.

"Maggie, what do you say we stop for something to eat? I don't know about you, but I didn't get lunch, and I'd like to discuss today's incident."

She looked up into his eyes and nodded, unable to speak.

He dropped his hands from her arms, and the sudden lack of heat sent a shiver through her body. "Why don't we go to Sally's Corner Kitchen? It's a nice, quiet restaurant on the edge of town. It's been open about a year or so."

Maggie followed Cody to a small restaurant situated in the corner of an L-shaped shopping complex. She hadn't been able to think of much other than Cassie's car and what the public vandalism implied. The person doing this was serious. Today's incident proved that he didn't care what he had to do to get to Maggie. Maggie had put her friend in danger. Granted, it was only a vandalized car, but the person had been bold enough to do it in broad daylight. What if it turned into more? The next line in the rhyme was regarding a boy. She couldn't bear it if something happened to Cody.

Sure, she wanted to hate him for hurting her like he had, but she couldn't. It didn't matter what he'd had done to her in the past, he did not deserve to be attacked.

Once inside, Cody led the way to a booth in the back corner where he sat with his back to the wall, facing the door. His gaze wandered around the entire restaurant, taking everything in. Just like she had read in her novels about police officers always wanting to keep an eye on their surroundings, she mused

The waitress took their drink orders and left them to peruse the menus.

"Sally's specialty is the chicken breast salad. She marinates a chicken breast in something, I've yet to figure out what, grills it to perfection, and places it on a bed of romaine lettuce. She will put anything on it you'd like. I take mine with carrot shavings, bell peppers, purple onions, and a boiled egg."

He hadn't even opened his menu. It sounded like he had already made up his mind. Maggie didn't know if she could eat. Guilt still gnawed at her stomach. "I'm not really hungry."

"You need to eat. It won't do for you to go without food."

He reached across the table and took her hand. She loved the feel of his holding hers, strong and steady. She was safe as long as he was there. Warmth slowly crept up her arm straight to her heart. She knew Cody would never have hurt her if he hadn't had a good reason. Maybe she should let him explain. In retrospect, she was more upset about the fact that he hadn't thought, whatever his reason was, that she should have a say in a decision that involved them both.

She gently pulled her hand away and looked down at it, placing the other one where Cody's had been in an attempt to capture the heat for as long as she could. When she spoke, it was barely above a whisper. "I know I need to eat. I think I'll try that salad."

Using his index finger, he raised her chin until she was looking at him, "Maggie, can we talk about that night?"

His features were soft and compassionate, his square jaw covered in stubble and his blue eyes dark with emotion. Before he could continue, the waitress delivered their sweet teas, took their order, and bustled back to the kitchen.

Her stomach clenched. She didn't want to hear about her shortcomings, especially in public. She changed the subject instead. "Cody. You said that the next couple lines in the rhyme were 'three for a girl' and 'four for a boy'. We now know that he chose to go after a close girl friend of mine. I'm afraid the boy will have something to do with you." Realizing he might read more into her statement than she wanted him to, she quickly added, "You're the only guy I know more than an acquaintance in town. I'd think it would possibly have something to do with Jacob, but he's away on business, so I figure he's safe."

"Maggie, before I got the call about Cassie's vandalized car, I talked to Alpha Security. Jake's job ended a couple days ago. They didn't need him as long as they thought, and they sent him home. I've called and left a couple of messages, and he hasn't returned any of them."

"That's what he does when he comes off a job, especially if it's high profile. He likes to spend a day or two decompressing and coming off the adrenaline high. I figured that would be something you knew already."

"Actually, we haven't talked much in the last six years."

"Oh," was all she could say. They had been inseparable in their teens. She'd assumed they'd stayed in touch.

"Maggie, the truth is, I couldn't face Jake after that night. I knew if I did, he would figure out I was the one you were dating and had broken your heart."

They hadn't told Jacob about their relationship. At first it had been weird, dating his best friend and keeping it a secret. She'd been afraid Jacob would be upset. He was fiercely protective of her, and Cody hadn't exactly been the upstanding teenager Jacob would've wanted her to date. He couldn't see the man Cody was becoming. It had been easy not to tell him. Being away at basic training and then stationed a hundred miles away, Jacob was hardly ever home.

Cody's truck pulled up the drive. After killing the engine, he stared fixedly out the windshield, straight at her sitting on the porch step.

Something was wrong, his jaw was tense. She walked to the truck. He watched her, never bothering to get out. His eyes were hard and intense. She knocked on the window. He seemed to come out of whatever trance he'd been. His features softened, and the storm in his eyes dissipated. He gave her a weak smile. He must have had another fight with his mom.

He opened the door and stepped out. She threw her arms around his neck, leaned up, and planted a small kiss on his lips. He responded by wrapping his arms around her and drawing her closer. He ran his hand up her back and tangled his fingers in her hair. He kissed her like he'd never kissed her before, like he was on the verge of dehydration and she was his lifesaving water.

Her lungs burned, and she pulled back, gulping for air.

"Whoa," she whispered, then looked around, hoping her dad and Jacob hadn't seen that. Cody had never kissed her in view of the house. And that had been way more passionate than they would have liked, she was sure. Not exactly the best way to tell her family about their relationship.

He leaned his forehead on hers. "Can we go for a walk before we go in?"

Still breathless, all she could do was nod. He reluctantly let her go and grabbed her hand.

Finally finding her words, she said, "We can't be too long, or they'll know something is up."

They walked to her mother's flower garden and took a seat on the stone bench. The muscles in his jaw constricted again. That hard look from before was back, making her uneasy.

"Is something wrong?"

"No. Yes." He let go of her hand and stood abruptly. His face was a mixture of pain and grief. He ran his fingers through his hair before shoving his hand in his already full pocket. What did he have in there?

Just for a second, she saw a fleeting glimmer of hope in his eyes. It disappeared as quickly as it came. Her heart sped up. He was beginning to scare her. "What is it?" She reached out to grab his free hand. He jumped back out of her reach. Her heart beat against her rib cage.

"I can't do this."

He was scared, that was all. Her pulse slowed, and she smiled. "Relax. They're not going to kill you. Maim you maybe."

She stood and took a step closer. He took a step back in response. "No. Not just that."

She didn't understand what he was talking about. "Then what can't you do?"

He looked down at his feet and back to her. Using his hand, he gestured between them. "This. I can't do this anymore."

He was breaking up with her. He couldn't be. There was no way this was happening. They were supposed to eat dinner with her dad and Jacob. They were going to finally tell them. "You said you loved me."

His face was hard, and his eyes were empty of emotion. "I lied."

Roaring filled her ears, and her heart exploded in her chest. She started gasping for air. No matter how much she gulped, she couldn't stop the burning in her lungs. She shook her head, denying the unthinkable.

"I love you!" Tears streamed down her cheeks. She didn't bother to wipe them away.

"Good-bye, Magpie." He turned around and marched to his truck, never looking back.

She numbly followed, hoping it was all a dream. His truck speeding down the drive, leaving her in a cloud of dust, broken and alone, proved it wasn't.

"Earth to Maggie?"

Cody had obviously been saying something to her, but she was lost in the memory of that night. "I'm sorry. I was thinking about something."

Cody's square jaw tensed. After a brief moment, he opened his mouth like he was about to say something but luckily, Maggie was saved by the waitress again. She placed their salads in front of them. Maggie made herself busy pouring the ranch dressing, hoping Cody wouldn't continue with whatever it was he was about to say.

"Shall I say grace?" Cody asked.

She nodded, glad that in the six years since she'd been away Cody hadn't lost his faith. Cody blessed the food and asked for continued protection and guidance in the coming days.

They ate in silence. The whole meal was awkward. There wasn't the normal friendly banter that had once graced their mealtimes. She missed those moments. She missed Cody.

"Maggie, I really don't think you should go home tonight."

"Why not? I've changed all the locks and added alarms to the windows." She turned her hands up in a questioning gesture.

"I'm glad that you did all those things, but what if he comes back? You're out there all alone. It'll be fifteen to twenty minutes before help could get to you."

"I have dad's old gun. I could take care of the immediate threat and then call the authorities. I want to go home. I have so much work to do, and I'm not going to get it done if I'm not there."

"I can't make you leave the house, can I?" She shook her head in response. "I'll come check things out then."

"You know it's not really necessary for you to see me home. I'm sure it's out of your way. It's a twenty-minute drive from town."

He reached across the table and grabbed her hand. His gaze met hers. His eyes were hypnotizing. "I would really feel better if I could."

She knew that Cody's stubborn streak was exactly like hers, a mile wide. If she were truthful, she *was* slightly afraid of going to the house alone. If she could make it one more night, the security company would be out tomorrow to install the security system. "Okay."

Letting go of her hand, Cody picked up the check the waitress had left and then threw a five-dollar bill on the table for a tip. "Dinner is on me tonight."

"You don't have to do that," she protested.

"I know I don't have to. I want to." He led the way to the register.

NINE

The sun had set by the time they pulled into the drive. Cody stepped from his cruiser and met Maggie by the porch steps. "Thank you," she said.

Cody could sense unease in her quiet voice as she wearily glanced over her shoulder to the large house looming in the dark. Was he causing the unease or was it being at the house alone? He was willing to bet that it was probably a mixture of both. Emotion flashed in her eyes, but before he could tell what it was, she turned and walked to the front door.

"You've seen me home. As you can see, it's all well. Have a good night, Sheriff."

He took the steps two at a time and gently grabbed her shoulder, turning her toward him.

"Please, let me go in and have a look around. It would make me feel a lot better about leaving you here if I know that the house is secure."

She nodded and handed him the keys. He unlocked the front door and walked into the entryway. He did a thorough search of the house, starting on the first floor and working his way up to the attic, checking the basement last. The house was clear. He made his way back to the living room where Maggie was staring out the front window into the dark night.

"Everything is clear."

"Thank you." She didn't bother to turn around. His gut clenched. Not being able to go on like this, her thinking the worse of him, he had to tell her the truth now.

"Maggie, I know you don't want to talk to me. I know that I hurt you that night. But I want you to know why."

She still didn't turn around.

Was she finally willing to listen? He took a deep breath, preparing himself.

"We were going to tell Jake about us later that night. But he had called earlier in the day. He wanted to have lunch and talk to me about something. I met him at Earl's Diner, and he said that he knew you were dating someone, that he could tell by how happy you seemed. I waited for him to say he knew it was me you were dating. I hoped he'd be giving his blessing, but he didn't. He had no idea it was me." He took a small step toward her and reached out to touch her shoulder but let his hand drop.

"He said he was worried. You had a full ride to Texas Tech, and you'd be the first one in the family to go to college. You were going to make something of yourself. You were going to go and do great things. He was afraid that your boyfriend would weigh you down, that you would either give up on college and stay here in Whitehaven or be so focused on the boy that you wouldn't meet your full potential. He talked about how he couldn't think of anyone in town that would be worthy of you." His chest constricted. He waited for her to respond. *Please say something. Say it's okay. Say you forgive me.* She didn't respond, though; she just continued standing there, absolutely still and quiet.

"All I could think about was that he was right. I wasn't the man for you. You deserved more than some boy whose father didn't love him enough to stick around and whose mother drank too much and found solace in the arms of any man who paid attention to her." He didn't want to go on. He knew his past, and he knew his future—both sad and lonely—except that one glorious year with her.

"I was never going to amount to anything. I wasn't in college. I was working at the sawmill outside of town. If you remember correctly, I was in trouble with the sheriff that summer we started dating. Sure, I straightened out, but still, I wasn't worthy of you." He had realized that Jake was right and decided to do the noble thing. He would sacrifice his happiness for her.

"You deserved someone so much more than me. I thought when I told you good-bye that night, I was freeing you. I was trying to make sure you would find the man that was worthy of your love."

She slowly turned around. Tear tracks lined her cheeks making her look as vulnerable as he felt.

"What about what I wanted? Did you stop to think about that? I knew about your past, I knew about your family, I knew about your job. None of those things mattered to me. You couldn't see what I saw. You couldn't see the man you were becoming. The man I loved. The man I had hoped I would spend the rest of my life with."

The ache in his chest intensified, constricting his lungs. He had to go to her. He could never stand to see her cry. It always broke his heart and made him feel so helpless. He took slow steps toward her, allowing her the opportunity to protest. When she didn't, he enveloped her in his arms, where she had been so many times before.

"I'm so sorry, Magpie." He held her a moment longer, inhaling the scent of strawberry vanilla shampoo that he loved. He stepped back and kissed her gently on the forehead.

She didn't flinch or tense. Maybe his confession was a step in the direction of healing their broken relationship. He felt lighter as hope renewed within him.

"Thank you." Her voice was barely above a whisper.

He reached out and brushed a lock of hair from her face, letting his fingers gently brush her check.

She stepped away from him. "I've listened to what you had to say. Now will you listen to what I have to say?"

He nodded. He wasn't sure where the conversation would go, or if he really wanted to hear what she had to say. He was afraid whatever it was would only break his heart further, but he owed her enough to listen.

"All these years, I thought I was the flawed one. That I wasn't good enough for you. That you dumped me because I wasn't what you wanted." Tears flowed freely.

"Oh, Magpie." He stepped forward to offer comfort, but she waved him off.

"Let me finish. I loath to admit it, but I allowed that night to affect me in such a great way. I lost faith in myself."

He grimaced as her words stabbed his chest. That hadn't been his intent.

"I had never let what anyone thought about me define me before. But it was different with you. I can't explain why. Maybe it was how our relationship had started. I had been drowning in despair after my mother's death, and you were there to help me see the light again. You had thrown me a life preserver. You showed me that there were still so many great things."

She crossed her arms over her chest and stared off to the right. "You reminded me of some verses in Ecclesiastes 3. *To everything there is a season, A time for every purpose under heaven: a time to be born, and a time to die.*" Her hand found its way to the cross that hung at the hollow of her throat. "*A time to plant, and a time to pluck what is planted; a time to kill, and a time to heal; a time to break down and a time to build up; a time to weep, and a time to laugh; a time to mourn, and a time to dance; a time to cast away stones, and a time to gather stones; a time to embrace, and a time to refrain from embracing; a time to gain, and a time to lose.*"

She looked him in the eyes, holding his gaze. He knew the verse and knew what was coming next. Guilt roiled in his stomach.

"A time to keep, and a time to throw away; a time to tear, and a time to sew; a time to keep silence, and a time to speak; a time to love, and a time to hate; a time of war, and a time of peace."

"I remember that. I drew you a picture of our favorite spot at the creek and wrote the first verse in calligraphy for you to keep as a reminder."

"I placed it in my Bible for safe keeping. After you ended things, I moped around in self-pity for a while. When it was time to leave for college, I hoped you would at least come say good-bye. But you didn't. My first few weeks of college were rough, but one night while I was reading my Bible I came across that picture and remembered. There was a time for everything. The time for love with you had come and gone, and I would start a new time. But first I would need to let go. And I did. Or I thought I had until I came back to Whitehaven."

He didn't know if he should be grateful that she hadn't let go. Her pain only intensified his, but there was a small glimmer of hope for him in her words.

"I'm so sorry. I never meant to hurt you. I know now that I should have talked with you first and not just dumped you. Hindsight is twenty-twenty. If I could take it back I would." He never imagined that his actions that night would have such a profound effect on her life.

"I wouldn't want you to."

He stared at her, knitting his eyebrows, shocked at her words. She admitted he'd caused her great pain, but she wouldn't want it taken back? Why would anyone welcome pain? He was sure he would prefer to live without it.

"Everything that I've gone through, every pain and joy that I've felt, all of my experiences have made me the person I am today." She closed the distance between them and grabbed his hand. "I forgive you."

73

A huge weight was instantly lifted from his chest. He was free for the first time in a long time. "You do?"

"Yes. Colossians 3:13 says, *'Bear with each other and forgive one another if any of you has a grievance against someone. Forgive as the Lord forgave you.'* Now. If you don't mind. I'd like to be alone."

"Thank you." He bent over and lightly kissed her cheek before stepping back. "I still don't think you need to be alone out here. Especially after today."

"I know how you feel, but I've taken every precaution to make sure I'm safe. The security company will be here tomorrow, and I'll be getting a state of the art alarm system. Besides, you being here isn't going to deter whoever is doing this. Remember they took a shot at both of us?"

"Yes, but at least I could slow them down a bit."

"I'm fine. There's no need for you to sleep in your car in the drive tonight. Thanks for that, by the way."

He smiled wryly. She could read his thoughts. "Well, I'll leave the house, but I'm going to hang around outside for a bit."

She sighed before leading him to the door. "Good night."

"Good night."

He took the flashlight from his utility belt and clicked it on. He circled the house and garage, searching for any signs that someone had been there. Not finding any, he turned his attention to the forest line. He walked the perimeter, shining his light into the woods.

After he finished, he returned to his cruiser and climbed in. He sat there staring at the large, white house. Maggie had forgiven him. Incredibly, she seemed able to appreciate that the struggles she'd endured had gotten her to who and where she was now. The more he thought about it, the more he was able to apply that thinking to his life. Everything he had gone through, good and bad, had cumulatively developed the man he was today. If he hadn't grown up with an absentee father and drunken mother, he might not have been attracted to the stability of Jake's family and may never have met Maggie. And he may have not have gone into law enforcement, if he had not had such an example of how *not* to live.

Letting her go had hurt both of them. He hoped that he could eventually get over her and fall in love again. But, if he were honest, he still loved Maggie and didn't know if there would ever be a time he didn't.

Now that she had forgiven him, was there a possibility that they could rekindle what they once had? He hoped so, but first he had to catch whoever was after her.

He put the cruiser in reverse and backed up, turned around, and exited the driveway. He breathed a heavy sigh. Finally explaining his actions and getting the opportunity to apologize to Maggie had been freeing. But her confession of the negative impact his actions had had on her life grieved him deeply. He'd wanted to protect her, but by assuming that he knew best, he'd taken away her chance to decide for herself. That trust and respect, the ability to discuss things openly, should have been part of their relationship. He would take her words to heart and learn from them, making him a better person in the future.

TEN

She'd managed to doze on and off for a couple hours, but now she lay in bed listening to the orchestra of crickets and other night creatures. No sense in tossing and turning. She decided she might as well get up and get some work done.

She slid her feet into her duck slippers and shuffled to the bathroom, where she flipped on the bathroom light, covering her eyes from the blinding brightness. Her father's insistence that they have fluorescent lights in the small white bathroom made her giggle.

The bathroom was a good place to start, so she swung open the medicine cabinet and took in the medicines that lined the shelves. They ranged from pain relievers to antacid to a prescription of antibiotics. She grabbed that one first. Prescribed in January of 2014.

"Geez, dad, that's only four years old." She tossed it in the trashcan, along with several others, including the antacid whose expiration date was last year. "That's not too bad." It was amazing he lived as long as he had with all this expired medicine.

She grabbed a washcloth from the linen closet and retrieved the bleach cleaner from its home under the sink. After cleaning the shelves, she moved to the cabinet top. A familiar bottle caught her eye. She picked it up and unscrewed the lid, breathing deeply. Warmth filled her chest as nostalgia swamped her. Every memory of hugging her father and smelling his cologne collided in her mind.

"Definitely keeping this." She put the lid on and took it to her room. She spent the next hour sorting and cleaning. She had a pile of things to donate and gobs of things for the trash man. Her father never threw anything away.

Time for a break. She padded down the stairs, intent on going to the kitchen to get a soda pop. Some people had to have coffee first thing in the morning. Not Maggie. She needed an ice-cold soda pop. As her foot hit the bottom stair, a low moan cut through the quiet. It sounded like it came from the front porch. The hair on the back of her neck stood on end. Someone or something was here.

Perhaps it was a wild animal. That had happened on occasion—an injured raccoon or a laboring feral cat would hide under the porch and make all kinds of noises. She tiptoed to the front window to catch a glimpse of whatever it was, but she didn't see anything. Maybe her imagination was getting the better of her. She turned to go to the kitchen and heard it again. She dashed to the couch and grabbed the cordless phone from the cradle on the end table. She dialed Cody's number.

"Hey, Maggie. How are—"

"There's a moaning noise coming from my porch." She didn't give him time to finish what he was saying. "I didn't see anything. I thought maybe I had imagined it, but I heard it again." She could hear rustling in the background.

"Maggie, do not go outside. Go upstairs and get your father's gun. I'm on my way. I was already on your side of town, so I'll be there soon. Stay on the phone with me, okay?" His cheerful voice disappeared and was replaced by the professional tone she noticed he used when he was working.

"Maggie."

She whipped her head to the front door where the voice had come from. Goose bumps sprang up on her arms. The voice was vaguely familiar.

"Cody, I heard my name." The panic welling up inside of her was ready to burst.

"Magpie, I am on my way. Do as I said and go upstairs, please."

She paused.

"Maggie." The voice. It was Jacob's voice calling to her from the other side of the door. Her anxiety quickly deflated.

That was just like him. Trying to scare her. She remembered the time that he and Cody had lured her out the front door and she'd almost stepped on a dead snake they had placed there to scare her.

"Cody, it's Jacob, it's his voice. Oh, I am going to kill him!" She stomped to the front door and disabled the alarm before yanking it open.

A blood curdling scream ripped from her throat, and the phone fell from her hand. She bent down in front of her brother's crumpled body. His hair was wild, and his clothes were torn and bloodied. Scratches and bruises riddled his exposed skin. She felt his neck for a pulse, it was there but shallow.

"Maggie!" Cody yelled from the phone. "Maggie. Answer me!"

She picked up the phone and tamped down the rising panic. "Cody, it's Jacob! He's hurt. He's bleeding. I need help!" Her heart raced, and her voice rose with each word.

"Maggie, I need you to calm down, okay? Can you take a deep breath for me?" He was in full cop mode now, trying to keep her calm. She wouldn't be any help to Jacob if she hyperventilated and passed out. She took a deep breath. And then another.

"Please, hurry," she whimpered.

"I am almost there. Can you tell me if he's breathing?"

She stared at Jacob's chest, seeing it rise and fall. "Yes, he's breathing."

"Do not hang up. I am going to set the phone down so I can radio for an ambulance and backup. I'll be right back."

She listened to him giving directions to his dispatcher. She didn't know what to do for Jacob, so she took his hand. He was covered in scratches and dried blood, but she couldn't see any open wounds. *Lord please be with Jacob. Let help get here soon. Keep him alive and heal his wounds. Amen.*

"Maggie, are you still there?" Cody's voice was back on the line.

"Please, hurry." Her voice sounded fragile.

"I'm turning on the drive now. I'm almost there. EMS is on their way."

The sirens were faint but grew louder. Cody's cruiser flew into the drive, sending dirt and gravel everywhere. He killed the sirens and tore from the car. He raced up the steps and knelt by her side, his attention fully on Jacob.

Bending over Jacob's lifeless body, Cody appeared to be listening for breaths. "Jake, it's Cody. Buddy, can you hear me?"

When he didn't respond, Maggie stifled a sob. *Lord, please let him be okay.*

Cody had reached to feel the beat of Jacob's pulse when he grabbed Cody's arm.

"Don't let her get Maggie." Jacob spoke hoarsely, never opening his eyes.

She reached out and touched Jacob's arm. "I'm right here." Her voice was equally as hoarse.

"Who? Don't let who get Maggie?" Cody prodded.

"Don't let her get Maggie." Jacob's hand released Cody's wrist and fell lifelessly to the porch. Cody reached to feel for a pulse.

Maggie gasped. "Jacob!"

Cody leaned back on his haunches. "Jake obviously couldn't have made it here by himself, so someone had to have dropped him off. That someone could still be here watching." His gaze roamed every inch of the property visible from the porch. Without taking his eyes off his surroundings, he spoke. "Maggie, go inside."

"But, I can't." She couldn't leave Jacob laying on the porch.

"Don't argue. Go inside. Now. Leave the door open so I can carry Jake in." The tone of his voice didn't leave room for argument.

Maggie did as she was told. Cody reached down, placed his forearms under Jacob's armpits, and lifted his upper body off the ground. He dragged Jacob into the house, never turning his back on the forest. Once they were in the house, Maggie shut and locked the door.

"I'm going to go get a wet washcloth." The tremble that was in her voice when she first found Jacob was gone. She was almost to the kitchen sink when Cody's booted footfalls echoed behind her, and then he grabbed her shoulder, stopping her from going any further. "What's wrong? Is Jacob—?" Emotion clogged her throat, and she couldn't even finish the sentence.

He rubbed his hands up and down her arms, trying to comfort her. "No, he's still breathing. I want you to stay away from all the windows. Jake was clutching a note. *Four for a boy.*"

Maggie's knees gave out, and she started to sink to the ground. She never hit the floor. Instead, she was scooped up and cradled to Cody's chest. He carried her to the couch, laid her down, and placed a throw blanket over her. She knew what he was doing, and she knew she needed to do something to help Jacob, but her body and mind were frozen. She couldn't move or speak.

"Maggie, you're in shock. I need to check on Jake, but I want you to stay here okay?" He stepped out of her line of sight.

The wail of sirens broke into the fog she was in. Thoughts whirled in her head. She couldn't lose her brother, too. He was all she had left. It wasn't long until paramedics were at Jacob's side. This was all her fault. Nausea rose up, and she took off for the hall bathroom. After flushing the toilet, she splashed cold water on her face.

"Maggie?" Cody knocked on the door. "Are you okay?"

Her stomach no longer ached, but her heart continued to do so. "Yes," she lied when she opened the door.

He pulled her close and walked her down the hall. "They're loading Jake into the ambulance. Go with them. I'll be there as soon as I can."

She finally got control of her body as Jacob was loaded onto a stretcher. She nodded to Cody, climbed up beside her brother, and rode in the ambulance to the hospital.

* * * *

She was tired of looking at the sterile white walls and equally ugly tile floors. The machine next to Jacob's bed beeped with each beat of his heart. It had been two hours since the ambulance had taken them away, and Cody still hadn't shown up. She couldn't explain why she needed him so much. She had called him out of fear. Cody, her protector, her comforter. Those were the things he had been before he had broken up with her.

She'd been in Whitehaven for three days, and she was already relying on him. She didn't want to. She didn't want to get hurt again. Yes, he'd explained why he'd dumped her, and he was sincere in his belief that he thought he was doing what was best for her at the time. He even seemed like he wanted to rekindle their relationship. But she wasn't sure if she was ready for that. Plus, she lived over a hundred miles away. Could a long-distance relationship really work? *What are you thinking? Your brother is laying in a hospital bed fighting for his life and you're thinking about love.*

She looked over at Jacob's unconscious body. "What happened to you?"

She remembered Cody stopping her before she'd made it to the kitchen sink. He'd said Jacob had been clutching a note. A note from her stalker. *God, please be with Jacob. Lord, heal his body. Bring him back to me. I can't lose him, too. Please.*

There was a light knock on the door. Cody stood in the doorway, looking like he'd aged ten years since she'd seen him this morning. She couldn't help herself. She jumped from the chair and ran to him. He wrapped his arms around her, and she buried her face in his chest. The floodgates opened, and sobs racked her body.

He didn't try to calm her like most people would. He held her and let her cry.

She wasn't sure how long he'd stood there and let her cry. She took several breaths, allowing her heart to slow before stepping back, instantly missing the warmth of his embrace. She swiped her hands across her eyes, drying her tears.

"Did you find anything?" She didn't look him in the eyes. She was sure they'd be full of compassion and that would cause another round of waterworks.

"Just like all the other incidents, we got nothing. We have no fingerprints, no trace evidence, nothing to go on. I'm beginning to think our guy has law enforcement experience or is a real CSI buff. But Jake called his assailant a she, so we could be looking for a woman. How is Jake?"

Slowly walking back to the chair she had vacated, she started to fill Cody in on Jacob's condition. "The doctor cleaned all of his wounds. He said most of them were superficial, like he had gotten them running through the woods. He does have some bruising around his wrists, as if he was shackled. His clothes were covered in dirt and sticks. The doctor said he would be saving them for you. He is severely dehydrated and suffering from exhaustion. He thinks Jacob has probably been in the wilderness for a few days. But he should make a full recovery."

Taking Jacob's limp hand in hers, she closed her eyes. *Why Lord? Why is this person doing this? Why is he hurting the ones I love?*

"Maggie, the security company came to install your new alarm system while we were processing the scene. I couldn't let them, since it was an active crime scene. You can't go back to that house. Not now. Not since this person has proven how dangerous he or she can be."

"I know. I'll consider a hotel here in town."

"I'm not sure that's a good idea, either. If this woman can get to your brother, a trained soldier and security expert, don't you think she can find out what hotel you're staying at?"

Where was she supposed to go? She didn't have anywhere else to stay. Cassie wouldn't hesitate to let her stay, but inviting her in would also be inviting more danger. She couldn't do that. "Where do you suggest then?"

"You could come stay at my house."

"That's not going to happen. It wouldn't be proper."

He was silent for a moment. He looked at his feet and sheepishly said, "We could make up a room for you at the sheriff's station."

"I do *not* think so. It's bad enough that this person has hurt people I love and sent me from my home. I will not let her turn me into a prisoner." Defiance coursed through her.

Jacob moaned, and her attention turned to him.

"Maggie," his rough voice whispered from the hospital bed.

"Shh, I'm here. Everything's all right." Tears filled her eyes as his hand tightened around hers.

"I... I..." Jacob tried to speak, but it seemed too difficult for him.

She gently squeezed his hand. "I'm right here. You're going to be all right. Just relax."

Cody took a tentative step toward Jacob's hospital bed.

"Cody's here, too." She gestured for Cody to come closer.

Jacob turned his head to Cody. "Keep her safe."

Jacob's eyes closed for a moment. She thought he had lost consciousness again, but then he opened his eyes. "Don't let her get Maggie."

Cody took Jacob's other hand in his. "I'm going to take care of her, as much as she'll let me anyway. But I need your help. Who is going to hurt her?"

Jacob's arm slackened, and Cody set his hand back on the bed gently. Clearly, he wouldn't be answering Cody's question anytime soon.

Maggie continued to hold Jacob's hand. Cody pulled up a chair on the other side of Jacob's bed, intent to sit and hold vigil with her.

The adrenaline slowly left her body, giving way to exhaustion. She laid her head on the edge of the bed and listened to Jacob's steady breathing. She was going to rest her eyes, just for a minute.

A tap on her shoulder startled her from sleep. She sat up, heart racing wildly. Cody was standing next to her. "Maggie, we should really go and get your stuff and get you squared away in a hotel. We can come back and check on Jake after we've gotten you settled. Okay?"

As much as she didn't want to leave, she knew Cody was right. She didn't have the truck since she had ridden in the ambulance with Jacob. She didn't have her purse, either, which contained her debit cards and identification, and she was going to need those to get a hotel room. It's a good thing she hadn't had a lot of time to unpack her travel bags. She didn't have anyone else to call, so with much trepidation, she agreed to let Cody take her to the house.

Before she left, she said another prayer over Jacob and gently kissed him on the forehead.

ELEVEN

Before they left the hospital, Cody assigned Deputy McKinley to watch Jake's room. He then contacted Deputy Grainger to have him come straight to the hospital instead of the station in the morning. Cody insisted that Maggie leave his phone number, in addition to hers, with the nurse. The drive was going to take at least twenty minutes. Now was as good as time as any to ask her questions about her life.

"Maggie, think real hard, is there anyone who could possibly have a reason to target you? Even the smallest oddity could hold the key to solving this. Are there any ex-boyfriends? Agitated coworkers? Angry parents? A neighbor who is holding a grudge?" He cast a sideways glance at her. She stared out the window, wringing her hands. Maggie had always been so kind. He couldn't imagine a reason anyone would want to hurt her.

"I've been thinking about this all morning. I haven't upset anyone that I know of. I adore my coworkers and the children. There are no issues there. And there haven't been any boyfriends, so we can cross that off."

Was Maggie's lack of boyfriends because of him? Could she possibly still have feelings for him? That thought gave him hope, but quickly deflated with the realization that maybe she didn't have any boyfriends because of how much he had hurt her.

"Cody, about what happened in the hospital." She paused. "I'm sorry. You know me, I'm not usually that emotional."

He placed his hand over hers and gave it a gentle squeeze in an attempt to calm her fidgeting. "It's understandable. A lot has happened, and a person can only take so much."

Unexpectedly, she didn't pull her hand away. That was progress, wasn't it? He could sit all day and revel in the feeling that she had forgiven him. Maybe she was putting the past behind them, but he needed to get back to reality. He needed to find out who was targeting Maggie. He pulled his hand from hers and placed it back on the steering wheel.

"After we get your stuff and get you settled into a hotel room, I'd like to sit down and talk this through some more. Maybe you can think of something once your mind settles a little."

He pulled the car into the drive and led the way into Maggie's father's house. Once he did a check of the house, Maggie went upstairs to gather her belongings.

He pulled out his cell to call in a favor while she wouldn't overhear what he was saying.

"Lone Star Inn. How may I help you?" Mary Lee, the clerk, answered on the second ring.

"Good afternoon, Mary. This is Sheriff Smith." He walked to the front window and looked out over the property.

"Well, hello, Sheriff. How are you this afternoon?"

"I'm doing well. And you?" He turned and looked around the living room.

"I can't complain."

"That's good. I've called to book a couple rooms. Do you have two connecting rooms available?"

"I do. Will this be billed to the county?"

"No, ma'am. This is personal." There had been a couple occasions where the county had had to rent rooms for various visiting professionals. "I'll be coming in with a young lady, probably within the hour. She's had some trouble at her house and needs a place to stay." He looked up the stairwell.

"I'll have them ready."

"Thank you." He hung up as Maggie came down the stairs with her bags.

He loaded the bags into the car, and they headed to the hotel. Fifteen minutes later, he pulled his car in to the parking lot of the Lone Star Inn.

The hotel was a small outfit. The rooms were all accessed from the parking lot. The office contained the check-in desk, kitchen, and breakfast area.

Maggie headed to the office, walked up to the service desk and rang the bell. Mary Lee came out from a small office. Mary had been working there for over thirty years. In recent years, Cody had had to come to the hotel on occasion in a professional capacity. Before that, he'd been the one who caused some ruckus, leading to the former sheriff being called.

"Yes, may I help you?" she asked Maggie, oblivious to Cody's presence.

"Mary," he interjected.

She looked at him and recognition dawned on her face. "Well, Sheriff Smith, I didn't realize this was the young lady you had spoken about on the phone. Your rooms are ready. Connecting doors like you asked for." She set the key cards on the counter.

He could feel the heat from the glare that Maggie aimed in his direction.

"Thank you, Mary. We'll go get settled in. Tell John I said hi."

He grabbed the cards and turned to Maggie, gesturing to the front door of the lobby. "Shall we?"

She let out a massive sigh and stomped off.

"We're in rooms two-oh-three and two-oh-four," he called as he chased after her. He wasn't in a hurry for the tongue lashing she was going to inevitably unleash, but she didn't need to be running outside without him. He caught up with her right after exiting the office. He took the lead and headed to the car.

Maggie grabbed her laptop from the front seat while he grabbed her two bags from the trunk.

"I don't need you to take care of me. Believe it or not, I am a big girl. I can carry my own bags." She grabbed one of the bags from his hand and huffed past him.

"I'm not taking care of you. I'm being a gentleman. I'm helping a lady to her room with her bags."

"Yes, a room that you paid for. A room that has an adjoining door to another room you paid for."

"Relax, will ya?" They climbed the stairs to the second-floor balcony walkway and continued to their rooms. He stepped around her to unlock the door. He was about to slide the key card in the door when she stepped in front of him. The top of her head barely reached his chin.

"You don't have to stay. You can send out another deputy." Her chin jutted out defiantly.

He leaned down, placing his hand on the door behind her head, and her breath hitched.

"I don't think this person is remotely close to done. I think he or she will come after you personally. *I* want to keep you safe." *I need to keep you safe.*

His gaze fell to her mouth. He wanted to close the distance and kiss her, to feel her soft lips on his, to make up for all the pain he caused and show her how much he loved her. She placed her hand on his chest. She filled his senses; the strawberry and vanilla was light and teasing, and the feel of her hand on his chest warmed his heart. Her hypnotizing green eyes searched his, and her lips parted just a hint. Was that an invitation? He needed to step away before he rushed into something she might not like.

He straightened and grabbed her hand from his chest, brushing a light kiss to her fingertips. "Now can we get settled in? We have time to go visit Jake if you'd like."

90

She nodded, curling her hand into a fist, like she was keeping his kiss. That simple action gave him hope.

He unlocked the door and walked into the small room. A queen-size bed was positioned up against the right wall with a small nightstand next to it. A flat screen television sat atop the dresser across from the bed. On the other side of the bed was a small breakfast table with two chairs and a door that led to a simple bathroom. A door next to the dresser would lead to his room, exactly like this, except mirrored in arrangement. It wasn't fancy, but it would work.

"I'm going to go next door and set my stuff down."

He set his things in his room and looked around. Finding the ice bucket, he went back to Maggie's room "I'm going to go fill this up, and then I'd like to talk some more about what's been going on. Don't open the door for anyone."

While at the ice dispenser, he purchased two soda pops from the machine conveniently placed next to the ice. He entered his room, removed the plastic wrap from two cups, and filled them with ice. Taking them to Maggie's room, he knocked on the doorframe of the open connecting door before entering.

"You still like soda, right?" He placed a cup and bottle in front of her before taking a seat at the table.

"Probably even more than I did before." She twisted the cap off the bottle and filled her cup. When the bubbles fizzed down, she took a drink.

"I know it's like beating a dead horse, but it's important that we try to figure out who is doing this. Can you think of anyone, anyone at all, who could be doing this? Jake indicated a woman was to blame for his injuries."

"I don't know who could be doing it." Her voice was strained.

"Are there any students who still failed after you had tutored them? Could a mom be upset with you? Are there any men who

91

have shown an interest in you and they felt rejected? Maybe a jealous ex-girlfriend of someone you dated?"

"No, none that I can think of. All the students I can remember were able to bring their grades up. They may not have been high grades, but they were better. And, no, like I said, no boyfriends. No dates. No jealous women."

She took another drink of her soda, and then her eyes widened. "Wait, there was one guy, Conrad Johnson. He had asked me out for dinner, and I agreed. We went out a couple times, but we didn't seem to click, at least not the way you and I had that summer." Maggie shrugged.

"So, you stopped seeing him? How did he take it?"

"Yeah. I told him how I felt and at first, I guess he seemed dejected. He asked a couple more times, but eventually he started dating someone else. I really don't think he has anything to do with this. He's married now, and his wife is expecting their first child any day now I believe."

"That's a place to start at least. Do you know her name? I'll have a deputy look in to them."

"Um, I think her first name is Stephanie. I don't know what her maiden name was." Maggie tried to stifle a yawn but failed.

He stood, gathering their trash. "I know you've had quite a couple days. I'll let you get some rest. I'll just be on the other side of the wall. If you need anything, all you have to do is knock."

"Actually, I'd really like to go see Jacob."

"We can do that." He knew she wouldn't really be able to rest until she was able to check on Jake again. He also hoped Jake would wake up again while they were there. The sooner they could get his statement, the sooner they could get this guy, or woman, before anything else happened. He had a feeling that the game was only beginning.

TWELVE

Her stomach rumbled, reminding her that she hadn't eaten supper last night. True to his word, Cody had taken her to see Jacob. The nurse had said his vital signs were good. Still, he remained weak and slept deeply the entire time they visited. She didn't want to leave him there alone, but Cody assured her that Deputy McKinley would remain outside his door throughout the night and then be relieved by Deputy Grainger. He was right; she couldn't do anything for him. And she needed to rest. The past few days were taking their toll on her. Not just physically, but mentally and emotionally as well.

Back at the hotel, after Cody had done another sweep of her room and left her for the night, she'd taken a hot shower and collapsed on the bed.

She'd woken in the morning feeling as though she'd only closed her eyes a second ago. When they checked in last night, she'd seen a sign in the lobby about their free breakfast. She made the bed, dressed in comfortable capri pants and a light cotton T-shirt, and slid the key card in her back pocket. Pausing by the adjoining door, she wondered if she should wait until Cody woke up. She decided against it. He was probably as worn out as she was. Plus, she was a big girl after all.

She opened the door to the parking lot to find Cody standing on the balcony with his arms resting on the railing, cradling a cup of coffee, and staring out into the parking lot. His hair brushed the collar of his shirt, which was a light green and fit snuggly across his broad shoulders.

"Good morning, sunshine. Going somewhere?" He turned and leaned against the railing, crossing his jean-clad legs at the ankles.

"As a matter of fact, I am. I'm headed for breakfast."

"I'll go with you." He took a sip from his coffee.

"I think I can handle eating by myself."

"Maggie, don't forget what's been going on. I really don't want you going *anywhere* alone. It's not safe."

Like she had forgotten what had happened. *Seriously though, what would it hurt to have breakfast?*

"Let me grab my room key, and I'll go down with you. I need to tell you about what could happen."

Before she could argue, he disappeared through his hotel door that he had propped open. He wasn't gone long before he stepped out and let the door shut behind him. "Shall we?" He offered his elbow like they were on their way to some fancy meal. She declined and walked ahead.

Once in the breakfast room, Maggie took in all the various breakfast foods. There were muffins, croissants, cereal, oatmeal, fruit, scrambled eggs, bacon, and more. She settled for a croissant with grape jelly, a helping of scrambled eggs, and a small bowl of fruit. Cody, on the other hand, filled his plate to the point she didn't think it would hold anything else.

They sat, and Maggie bowed her head. *Lord, thank You for Your love and saving grace. Be with Jacob and continue to heal his injuries. Be with us and keep us safe in Your protection. Be with Cody and his deputies as they search for the person behind this. Amen.*

When she looked up, Cody's head was bowed in a silent prayer of his own. She was staring when he finished, and their gazes locked. She could feel heat beginning to color her cheeks. He gave her a grin, causing his eyes to sparkle.

94

"Oh, I forgot something." He went back to the breakfast bar. For what, she couldn't imagine. She had no idea where he was going to put all the food already on his plate.

She was busy spreading jelly on her croissant when Cody placed a chocolate muffin in front of her. He pulled a candle and a box of matches from his pocket, stuck the candle in the muffin, and lit it.

He sat down and started to sing the birthday song. His baritone voice was swoon worthy. It reminded her of those old-time crooners. She'd always loved to hear him sing. Her face was on fire, and all she could do was stare at him. He remembered her birthday.

"Happy birthday, Magpie."

"Thank you."

"Go on. Make a wish, "

She made a show of making a wish and blowing out the candle. He laughed. It was a sound that she could never get tired of hearing.

"What did you wish for?" He winked

"Now, I can't tell you that or else it won't come true." She took a sip of her drink to stifle the giggle that was rising.

Geez, what was she, a teenager? She shouldn't be sitting here enjoying this moment with her brother laid up in the hospital and some crazy person after her. She sighed deeply and placed her cup back on the table. Picking up her fork, she stabbed a small piece of cantaloupe and popped it in her mouth. Cody ate in silence for a few minutes, then sighed heavily, sat back, and rested his hands on his thighs.

"Like I said, we need to talk about where this situation could wind up. I keep thinking that the person stalking you could be related to the first case I worked as sheriff. Iris, one of our dispatchers, started receiving flower deliveries with little poems written on the cards. She chalked it up to a secret admirer. Then one day she received a single flower and a box."

He took a deep breath before continuing. "Inside the box was a threatening note. No more sweet words. After that first note, she'd find more notes. Sometimes under her windshield, taped to her door, sent to her email, she even received texts. One day she opened her refrigerator and found a note taped to her milk jug. She did the smart thing and had all of her locks changed and called a security company to install a security system."

Cody paused, taking a drink from his orange juice. *Poor Iris.* Maggie could understand a portion of what she must have felt. While their cases weren't identical, they were certainly too similar to be a coincidence. She ate another piece of cantaloupe.

"The next morning, she woke up to find roadkill had been thrown on her porch. More gruesome deliveries arrived. Her brother, Deputy Grainger, moved in with her. He thought she would be safer if he stayed with her. She was never alone. She'd become a prisoner."

He fidgeted with his fork, moving some of his food around on the plate. "We watched her withdraw from the world, from her friends. She'd been a happy outgoing person, but her stalker changed that. I worked every angle on that case. There were no clues, no forensic evidence, no suspects. I had nothing. I felt so helpless."

She didn't like that he blamed himself. Reaching across the table, she grabbed his hand, "Cody, you said you'll be with me all the time. I'll be safe."

He placed his other hand over hers. "See, that's the thing. Iris's story doesn't end there. One day while Grainger was in the shower, there was a knock on the door. Iris looked out the peephole and saw that it was a postal service worker with a package. She thought it would safe to open the door."

He stared over her shoulder for a brief moment. "When Grainger got out of the shower, Iris was gone, and the front door was wide open. We found her an hour a later, unconscious on a bench at the city park. She was alive, but she had been drugged. Thankfully, she hadn't been assaulted, but she did have a mark to show how close her stalker had gotten. He had used some sort of branding iron and burned a mark into her collar bone."

The cantaloupe she had eaten turned to lead in her stomach. He gently squeezed her fingers. "That's why I want you to be vigilant. Anything can happen. Even when you think protection is close. I couldn't protect Iris. I couldn't even find the person responsible. Knowing that she eventually ended her life because I couldn't do my job right is even worse. If something happened to you—" He swallowed hard and looked away. His Adam's apple bobbed, and he blinked several times before looking back to her, "I don't know what I would do."

Overcome with compassion for the man sitting across from her, Maggie reached over the table with her free hand and used her fingertips to turn his face to her. She cupped his chin between her forefinger and thumb. "You, Cody, are not responsible for what Iris did. You remember that. She made that decision. Just because you couldn't find the person responsible for tormenting that poor woman does *not* mean you are not a good sheriff. If you treat all your cases like you have mine, then you're the best sheriff Dale County could ask for. I promise I'll be careful, and I'll make sure not to take off without you."

He reached up, took her hand in his, and placed a gentle kiss on her palm. His soft lips sent butterflies fluttering through her.

"Thank you for that." He let go and took a drink. "I thought we could go see Jake. Maybe he'll be awake."

"I'd like to see him. Something I don't understand is Jacob is a trained soldier and a security expert. How could someone get the jump on him?" She'd thought about that when she couldn't sleep this morning. She took a bite of her croissant.

Cody was quiet, the look on his face told her he was thinking. "I've thought of that myself. Either they sabotaged him, or it was someone he knew. Unfortunately, we won't have an answer until he wakes up." He returned to his breakfast with gusto. Like her, he hadn't eaten last night. He looked as famished as she was.

She decided to save her chocolate muffin for last, and they ate the remainder of their breakfasts in relative silence. When she was finished, she peeled the wrapper from her muffin, and using a butter knife, she cut it in half. She scooted half to Cody.

He looked up at her. "It's your birthday. Eat up."

"What's the point of having birthday cake if you can't share it?"

"It's not exactly cake."

"The principle still applies."

He smiled at her before popping a piece of muffin in his mouth.

THIRTEEN

After breakfast, Cody escorted Maggie back to her room to get her purse. They were going to go see Jake. He hoped Jake would wake soon so he could shed some light on who had done this to him. With any luck, they'd be able to catch the person and put him behind bars. Today was Maggie's birthday. She deserved to be happy and enjoy this day, not worry about what some madman was going to do to her.

He'd had the idea of the birthday muffin while he was filling his plate at the breakfast bar. Miraculously, the kitchen had some candles. Maggie's expression when he'd placed it in front of her had amused him. It had been a mixture of shock and gratitude. He'd hated to ruin it discussing the horrible reality of what was happening and the possible connection to Iris's case.

It didn't take Maggie long in her room, and the drive to the hospital took five minutes. He parked in the parking garage, and they took the elevator to the floor where Jake was staying. The elevator doors opened, and Cody was surprised to see that it was Deputy Minton, not Deputy Grainger, stationed at Jake's door.

"Maggie, go on in. I'm going to talk with Deputy Minton for a moment."

She furrowed her eyebrows, then slowly opened the hospital room door and quietly entered Jake's room.

"I thought Deputy Grainger was on duty this morning?" Cody asked.

"He is. He called and asked me to fill in for him for a bit. He said he was on his way in, but his cruiser had a blowout."

"Has Jake woken up?"

"No, sir. Not yet anyway. The doctor hasn't made his rounds yet this morning."

Cody left Minton at the door and entered the room. Maggie sat next to Jake's bed, holding his hand, leaning close to his ear, whispering to him.

He leaned against the door, watching Maggie tenderly talk to her brother. They didn't deserve this. Cody wanted to find whoever was doing this and put them behind bars where they belonged.

Jake started moaning, and Cody closed the distance to the bed and stood next to Maggie. Jake opened his eyes and closed them just as quickly. He wrinkled his forehead and squeezed his eyes shut, then opened them again. "Magpie?" he whispered.

"I'm right here. And Cody's here, too." Joy filled her face as she reached up and grabbed his hand. Her touch made his heart skip a beat.

"Hey, Jake."

Jake took a moment to focus on Maggie's face, then turned to him. "Cody."

"Hey, Jake. Nice having you awake." Cody let go of Maggie's hand, pulled up a chair, and sat next to the bed.

Jake looked back at Maggie. "I'm so glad you're safe." His voice was strained.

"I'm fine. See? Let me get the nurse and some water." She quickly left the room in search of her quarry.

"She told me Maggie had been in an accident. She said they were afraid she wasn't going to make it," he whispered hoarsely as he leaned his head back against the bed and grimaced. Cody's heart picked up pace. Jake had seen his attacker.

"Who told you that?"

"Your dispatcher. What's her name? Donna?"

Cody's eyes grew wide as he shook his head. Jake had to be mistaken; he must have hit his head. Dee couldn't possibly be involved. "Dee told you Maggie had been in an accident?"

Jake nodded and opened his eyes. "There was a message on my voicemail when I came off duty." He took a deep breath and swallowed a couple times.

"Dee said to call her. I did as soon as I could. She said Maggie had been in an accident. I told her when my plane would be arriving, and she said she'd meet me at the airport." Jake ran his hand over his face.

"What happened when she met you at the airport?"

"We got into her car. It had the Dale County parking pass hanging from the rearview mirror. We headed to the hospital. She offered me a bottle of water from a little cooler she had. I didn't think anything of it. The last thing I remember, before coming to in the woods, was drinking that water. She must have drugged me." Jake brought his arm down and slammed it on the bed. The action caused a groan to escape from his lips.

"I woke up in the woods, chained to a tree. I yelled, hoping someone would hear me. I tried to get the chains off my wrists, but when that didn't work, I tried to break them. It was no use; I couldn't get free. I waited, hoping someone would come eventually. I was out there for two days. I guess I finally passed out because I don't remember anything until waking up here."

The two days prior to finding Jake had been two of the hottest days yet. It would have only been a matter of time before Jake had become dangerously dehydrated to the point of unconsciousness. Dee must have waited until he passed out before moving him to Maggie's porch. He didn't think Dee capable of something like this. She didn't even know Maggie. How could she possibly be the one targeting her?

Maggie came back in the room with a cup of ice water and a nurse following on her heels.

"Well, good morning, Mr. Jones," the nurse said brightly as she walked over to his bedside to assess his vitals.

This would be the perfect opportunity for Cody to excuse himself and have someone go pick up Dee. It was her day off, so she wouldn't be at the office.

Deputy Minton was still standing outside the door. Cody walked down the hall to find a private place to talk. He didn't want to have this conversation in front of Minton, in case Jake was mistaken. He pulled his phone from his pocket and dialed Deputy Grainger.

"Yes, Sheriff," Grainger answered on the second ring.

"Minton said you had a tire problem?"

"Yeah, I did. It's all changed, and I'm on my way to the hospital now."

"I have something else for you. Jacob Jones woke up. He says Dee is the one responsible for his injuries."

"Dee? You're kidding, right?" Grainger sounded as surprised as Cody.

"I'm afraid not. I need you to go pick up Dee and bring her in. I'm going to stay here and see if I can get anything else from Jake. Do not question her. Call me once you have her in custody, and I'll meet you at the station."

"Yes, sir."

Cody ended the call and put his phone in his pocket. Could this be his fault? Was Dee trying to hurt him because he hadn't wanted to start a relationship with her last year? Surely not. He'd heard her and Angie, the third shift dispatcher, talking last week about her new boyfriend. She hadn't said his name, but she seemed genuinely happy. He went back to the hospital room, hoping to get more details from Jake.

"Cody, Jacob says Dee is the one who did this to him. Is that true?" Maggie asked with wide eyes.

102

"I've got Grainger going to pick her up now. We'll get to the bottom of this."

"I've never met Dee. Well, not until I saw her the other day. I can't even begin to imagine what the woman would have against me."

"I know." He moved closer to the bed. "Jake, can you describe the woman who picked you up? I know you said she told you her name was Dee, but what did she look like?"

Jake closed his eyes as if he were checking a memory bank. "She was about a foot shorter than me. I'd say one hundred twenty pounds. Brown, shoulder-length hair and brown eyes."

"That sounds like Dee." He pulled his phone from his pocket and scrolled through some photos. He stopped on a photo of a kindergarten class that had come to visit the station. Several deputies outlined the group. Dee was mixed in with them. He turned the phone to Jake. "Do you see her here?"

Jake squinted and studied the picture. "That's her." He pointed to the woman to the left of Deputy Minton. Dee. He put the phone back in his pocket.

"Do you remember which way she drove out of the airport?"

"She drove..." Jake closed his eyes, and as the silence stretched, his breath started to even out.

"Cody, he's exhausted. Maybe we should let him rest," Maggie whispered so as not to wake Jake.

"You're right."

They spent a few more minutes sitting there quietly before leaving. He hated to leave without more details, but Jake needed his rest. Cody lead the way to the elevators. The elevator dinged their destination as his phone rang. "Sheriff Smith."

"Sheriff, Dee's not at her house."

"I was afraid of that. Stay there and see if she comes back. I don't want to put an all-points bulletin out over the radios just yet. It'll let her know that we're on to her."

"I agree. I'll sit here and grab her when she comes home."

"Good." He disconnected the call, got in the car, and started it. He rested his hands on the steering wheel and leaned his head against the headrest. After a moment, he shifted his body so he was facing her. "Maggie, I'm sorry about this. If Dee is responsible..." He paused, laying his hand on the console. "I had no idea." Anguish filled him as thoughts swirled in head. Why would she do this?

Maggie put her hand on his, stopping his fingers from drumming and pulling him from his thoughts. "How could you know? I'd never met her until that day in your office."

He turned his hand over and intertwined their fingers. Their hands fit together perfectly. The old feelings were starting to bubble to the surface. First, he'd kissed her fingertips at the hotel, then he'd kissed her palm at breakfast, and now he was holding her hand. He wanted nothing more than to go back to the way they once were.

"You wouldn't have met Dee. She moved to town about two years ago."

"Why would she target me?

"All I can think is she might be targeting you because of me. Before I was Sheriff, she'd shown interest in me, beyond that of a coworker. I told her I wasn't interested in a relationship at the time. She asked for at least a shot. I agreed. We went out a couple of times, but I had no interest in extending our relationship. She was disappointed at first, even avoided me for a few weeks, but she eventually moved on. It's hard to believe though. I never would have thought she was bitter or resentful, much less violent."

"There are things that have happened, details that she wouldn't know anything about unless you told her. Was I your dinner conversation? Did you go on dates and tell them about poor, pitiful Maggie?" She crossed her arms over her chest.

"Come on, Maggie. It's not like that at all. I never talked about you. Not to Dee, or to any other dates for that matter. I don't know how she knew those things, but I think if Jake said she's the one that drugged him, then she is."

"So, what do we do now?"

He put the car in reverse. "*We* don't do anything. When Dee decides to go home, Grainger will bring her in, and then I'll get to the bottom of this. In the meantime, I will stick close to you and make sure you're safe."

She seemed to finally be accepting his comfort and protection, which would make his job easier. But she was much more than just a job to him. They'd had a romantic history together and had known each other even longer than that, and he wanted to get all of that back.

"Cody, it's really not necessary. You don't have to personally babysit me. What about Deputy Grainger or one of your other deputies?"

"I'm not leaving you alone, so get used to my presence." He was pretty sure she was trying to put some distance between them, but he wasn't going to leave her with anyone else until this was over.

"Don't you have some important sheriffing to do?" She was trying to find an escape.

"This is important sheriffing. Is that even a word?" He raised his eyebrows.

"It is now." She sighed. "Cody, I've got so much that needs to be done at the house. Can we go back there?"

"I know this is not what you had planned and it's putting you behind schedule, but it's really best you lie low, until we have Dee in custody."

"I can't sit cooped up in a hotel. I feel like a prisoner, and I haven't done anything wrong. I know you told me about Iris and how her case turned out, but I'm not Iris. Could we at least run to Jacob's and get some of his clothes and toiletries?"

"Sure. I don't see the harm in getting some of Jake's things and taking them to him… Maggie, I know this is a miserable situation. I know you hate being cooped up and threatened, and I get that spending so much time with me doesn't exactly make it easier. But, you've got to realize, if Dee is the perpetrator, we're talking about someone who has law enforcement training. I don't want you taking any chances. So, restricting your activities will make it easier to keep you safe."

* * * *

They collected some of the necessities for Jake and spent the afternoon visiting with him in the hospital. When the doctor came in, he'd spoken optimistically of the possibility of Jake being released the next day. Cody hoped that was true, both for Jake, and because it was plain that Maggie was drowning in guilt and concern over Jake's hospitalization. The ride back to their hotel was silent. Maggie sat in the passenger's seat, forehead against the window. Cody pulled into the parking lot and killed the engine as his cell phone rang. "Grainger, tell me you got Dee in custody."

"No such luck. She hasn't come back yet. I was thinking maybe I could drive around town and look for her car."

"It couldn't hurt. If she's figured out we know, she's not gonna come home, especially if she recognizes a deputy's car staking out her place."

"I'll drive around. I'll call if I find her."

"Call for back up if you need to, then call me."

"Ten-four." Grainger disconnected the call.

Cody turned to Maggie. "Let's go inside."

They climbed the stairs to their floor. Pulling the key card from her back pocket, she stuck it in the slot. Before she could pull it out, he wrapped his hand around hers.

"Maggie, let me go first."

Wearily, she pulled the key card out and let Cody enter the room first. He stepped over the threshold. Walking through the room, he looked in the closet, bathroom and even peeked under the bed. He wasn't going to take a chance. Satisfied her room was safe, he opened the adjoining door and disappeared into his room, checking it.

Maggie sat at the table, head resting on her folded arms. When he returned, he reached out and squeezed her shoulder. His attempt to offer support backfired, though. She jolted straight up.

She felt so close to tears, his affectionate gesture almost broke her. The fear and worry had made her brittle—emotionally vulnerable. If she wasn't careful, she would throw herself into his arms, her heart his for the taking. She had to keep her distance.

"I know this week has been rough, Magpie. Definitely not your best birthday, but I promise after this is all over, I will make it up to you with lots of balloons and a giant cake."

"Honestly, I'd rather just forget this whole summer." She stood and walked to her overnight bag, pulling out clothes.

"What can I do to help? You didn't have any dinner. How about I order us something?"

"I'm not hungry." She walked past him and stopped at the bathroom door. "I'm going to take a shower, and then I'm going to go to bed… G'night."

FOURTEEN

Cody sat on the bed letting the television watch him. He'd turned it on intending to watch the ten o'clock news but instead got lost in thought. Maggie had been so dejected tonight, it had nearly broken his heart. She'd moved around the room so stiffly, as if a light breeze could break her. He prayed that a good night's sleep would help.

He thought of her cupping his face, defending him fiercely against his own guilt. And he remembered their fingers intertwined as they sat together in the car. Despite her continued distance, he felt she was slowly warming back to him.

Sudden pounding on the door between their rooms, along with Maggie's muffled voice, sent adrenaline racing through him, propelling him off the bed and to the door. No sooner did he have the door open than Maggie was in his room. In pajama pants and a t-shirt, she was fresh from the shower, damp hair flying loose around her face.

Her eyes were full of fire. "She's been here. Dee was in my room."

"What do you mean? Everything was fine when I did a walk-through. I even looked under the bed. I didn't see any signs that someone had tampered with anything."

"Yeah, well, she left me a present under the blanket! Go in and take a look for yourself." She waved her arms wildly in the direction of her room.

He entered the room and could immediately see something dark contrasting with the crisp white bed sheets. Loose black rose petals and a dark gooey substance that spelled out the next line of the rhyme. *Five for silver.* A simple white card lay to the right of the creation. Taking his multipurpose tool from his pocket, he used the plier portion to open the card. *Here lies one whose name was writ in water.*

What does that mean? This isn't water.

He wasn't going to stick around to find out. He grabbed Maggie's shoes and took them with him to his room. "We need to leave. I'll call someone to contain the scene once we're on the road." He barked as he handed her shoes to her. "Did you touch anything other than the blanket?"

She sat on the edge of the bed and shoved her feet into her shoes. "No, I'm not stupid." The tone of her voice indicated she thought his order barking and question had been uncalled for.

"I'm sorry, I didn't mean it that way. Did you see what was written on the card?"

"No, I saw the mess and came straight to your room. I didn't stick around to see what sick note she left." She stood and marched to the door, but before she opened it, she turned to him, deflated. "I don't have anywhere else to go. I'm not sure I really want to run again. I mean, she's just going to follow me until she's caught. Maybe if we stay here, she'll come back, and you can arrest her, and this thing will all be over."

"I think Dee is too smart for that."

He grabbed his belt, containing his holster and gun, and put it on. Grabbing his wallet, keys, and cell phone from the dresser, he met her at the door. "I'm going to keep you safe. We have to pray and ask God to help us end this." He squeezed her shoulder.

"What about my stuff?"

"We'll get it later. There's no telling if Dee is still here and whether or not she's left any other surprises in your room." He motioned for her to step behind him as he slowly opened the door and cautiously took in the surroundings. There wasn't a soul in the parking lot or anywhere he could see. He stepped out onto the walkway and told Maggie to stay behind him. They quickly made it to his car. He started the engine and wasted no time leaving the parking lot. He pulled his cell from his pocket and dialed the station.

"Dale County Sheriff's office, this is Angie."

"Hey, Ang, it's Sheriff Smith."

"Hey, Sheriff, it's a little late for a call from you."

"Yeah, well, I need you to alert Whitehaven PD about another crime scene at the Lone Star Inn connected to Maggie Jones. Someone got in and left Maggie a message. She was in room two-oh-three."

"Yes, sir."

He hung up and started going over the latest note in his head.

"Maggie, the rhyme was *five for silver*, but the card said, 'Here lies one whose name was writ in water.' Do you know what that means? Do either of them make sense, either together or separately?" Based on her silence, he assumed she didn't. "I'm also pretty sure that the gooey substance was blood."

She didn't flinch or take a sudden inhalation of breath like he would expect her to. She was becoming used to this. A memory of Iris's undaunted reaction to the last note flashed in his mind. He had to find Dee; he couldn't let Maggie get to the point that Iris had. The sound of her voice whispering toward the window pulled him back to the moment.

"When I have fears that I may cease to be,
before my pen has glean'd my teeming brain,
Before high-piled books, in charactery,
Hold like rich garners the full ripen'd grain;
When I behold, upon the night's starr'd face,

111

Huge cloudy symbols of a high romance,
And think that I may never live to trace,
Their shadows, with the magic hand of chance;
And when I feel, fair creature of an hour,
That I shall never look upon thee more,
Never have relish in the faery power
Of unreflecting love—then on the shore,
Of the wide world I stand alone, and think,
Till love and fame to nothingness do sink."

"What is that?" He reached over and touched her arm, afraid she was going into shock and rambling nonsense.

She turned to face him. *"When I Have Fears that I May Cease to Be* is a poem by John Keats."

He looked at her blankly. *What does a poem have to do with what I asked her?* "I don't get it."

"John Keats was a poet that lived in the late eighteenth and early nineteenth centuries."

He cocked an eyebrow at her and then returned his attention to the road. "I'm still not following. I don't need a literature lesson right now."

"'Here lies one whose name was writ in water' is engraved on his tombstone."

"Oh, okay. So, what does a poet who died three hundred years ago have to do with you?"

"Keats contracted tuberculosis, a nasty disease that eventually led to coughing up blood and death. He died when he was twenty-five. Today is my twenty-fifth birthday. I guess Dee wanted to be clever." A single tear slid down her cheek.

Without thinking, he pulled the car onto the shoulder, reached over the console, and pulled her into his arms. For a moment, she sat there, rigid and uncomfortable. Just when he was about to let go, she relaxed into his embrace. He rubbed her back, willing his strength to her.

He had seen Grainger doing the same thing for Iris when she'd endured taunting notes and veiled threats. She had even been physically attacked. Through it all, Iris had been strong, not showing a lot of emotion. He had admired the strength he thought she had had... that is until he found the note next to her lifeless body.

He shook the image from his mind. He would not let Maggie get to that point. He would find Dee and end this horrible game.

He closed his eyes and rested his cheek against her soft hair. "Lord, give Maggie strength. I pray for protection. For not only Maggie but for everyone involved. Lord let us find Dee and get her the help she needs. Amen."

"Amen," she whispered against his chest before pulling out of his arms and leaning into her seat, resting her head on the headrest. Turning to Cody, she gave a weak smile. "Thank you."

"I'm not sure what you are thanking me for, but you're welcome."

"For being here, and for helping me."

"Anything for you, Magpie." He reached across the console and squeezed her hand. He didn't let go immediately.

She moved her hand, breaking the connection and wrapped a loose curl around her index finger and started twirling it.

"I guess we'll go back to my house." He put the car in drive and merged back onto the deserted road.

"We've already been through this, Cody. I'm not going to stay at your house." Exasperation filled her voice.

"Stubborn as ever. Where else do you suggest?"

"I can go stay at Jacob's house. He's still in the hospital, and I'm sure he won't mind."

He shook his head. "I don't like it. Dee knows where your brother lives. We can't risk going somewhere she could find you.

That also means all the resources of the Dale County Sheriff's office are out, too.

"Well, see, then going to your house wouldn't be a good idea, either." She crossed her arms over her chest, claiming her small victory.

"You're right. It's after midnight. I think we should go to a hotel in one of the neighboring towns. I can call Grainger from there."

She leaned back into the car seat and closed her eyes.

Cody drove them to the Tumbleweed Inn, a small hotel set up much like the previous one, in Prairie's Grove, a city north of Whitehaven. He spoke with the night manager and checked them in under an alias. He was being careful. He had kept an eye on the rearview mirror the entire trip to make sure they hadn't been followed.

Their rooms were joined by a door like the last hotel. "I'll leave the adjoined door unlocked should you need anything." He made sure she was comfortable in her room before returning to his own. He had phone calls to make to find out what evidence—if any—the police had found in Maggie's hotel room.

FIFTEEN

After lying on the uncomfortable bed for what felt like hours, Maggie finally drifted to sleep, but it wasn't restful. She kept drifting in and out of consciousness.

Finally, after the second nightmare and a trip to the bathroom, she admitted defeat. She was wide awake. No matter how hard she tried, she couldn't go back to sleep. Rolling over, she looked at the clock on the night stand—6:15 a.m. She wasn't going to be going back to sleep anytime soon. Swinging her legs off the bed, she planted them firmly on the carpet and stretched her arms over her head, working the kinks from her back.

When she stood, she saw her reflection in the mirror hanging on the wall. A pale face with dark circles under her eyes, hair sticking up in all sorts of directions—the woman staring back at her was a stranger.

She rubbed the sleep from her eyes as she walked to the bathroom. After splashing cold water from the bathroom faucet on her face, she ran her wet hands over her hair trying to tame any flyaways as she gathered the unruly mess into a somewhat contained bun. She ran her tongue over her teeth and felt a thick coat of fuzz. Okay, she was mentally exaggerating, but she wished the hotel provided complimentary toothbrushes and toothpaste.

She walked to the adjoining door. It was no longer closed, but slightly cracked. He must have checked on her during the night. She stuck her ear to the door, listening for any noise. Silence. He must still be sleeping.

"You can come in." His voice startled her. She must not have been as quiet as she thought.

She pushed the door open. She didn't know what she expected, but it wasn't to see Cody sitting at the little breakfast table with an open Bible in front of him.

He hadn't looked up, so she took a moment to take in his relaxed features. The tension that had been radiating off him for the past couple of days was absent. His blond hair swept just above his eyebrows, masking the scar he had gotten from one of his and Jacob's rough games of basketball. The circles under his eyes were slightly darker than hers. His face was beyond the five o'clock shadow stage and well on its way to a beard.

It suited him. He was no longer the fresh-faced teenager she'd fallen in love with. He was a rugged man full of strength and determination. One who would do anything to protect the woman he loved. Did he love her?

"It's rude to stare," his husky voice interrupted her appraisal.

"Uh, I'm sorry. I didn't mean to disturb you." She glanced at her feet, knowing her pale skin once again betrayed her embarrassment at being caught all but ogling him. "I couldn't sleep."

He shifted in his chair and ran his hand through his hair then turned his compassionate eyes to her. She held his gaze, noticing something hidden in his eyes. She couldn't quite figure out what it was, but before she could study them any longer, he cleared his throat and looked away. When he looked back at her, whatever had been hidden there was gone.

"Grainger called. A deputy was stationed outside of Dee's house last night while he looked around the area for her car. She never showed up. I've had them issue an APB on her. The substance in the bed was definitely blood. From the basic field test we can do, we know it's not human blood."

116

The news that Dee was still out there knotted in her stomach. Cody must have sensed her discomfort because he gestured for her to have a seat next to him at the table.

"I picked this Bible up off the night stand. I've heard it said that *do not fear* or *fear not* is in the Bible three hundred sixty-five times, one for each day of the year. I'm not sure if that's true, but I do know that Proverbs 18:10 says that *The name of the Lord is a strong tower, the righteous run to it and are safe.* I know right now is rough, Maggie. I know you've got to be afraid. But you can call on the Lord. He can give you peace and comfort in this time."

He took her hand and looked her in the eyes. "Can we pray?"

She nodded, unable to speak. He had quoted the exact scripture she had run across days ago while she was staying at her father's house.

He closed his eyes and bowed his head. "Lord, thank You for Your love and Your saving grace. Lord I pray that You will help us find Dee and put an end to her sick game. I pray that You will be with Maggie, Lord. I pray that You will wrap Your loving arms around her and give her the peace and comfort only You can. I pray that she will rely on You, that she'll know that You are here. Amen."

"Lord, thank You for sending Cody back into my life. I pray that You will be with Cody and his deputies as they search for Dee, Lord. Give them wisdom and keep a hedge of protection around them. Amen," Maggie added.

They sat silently at the table, studying each other. Still holding her hand, he used his free hand to tuck a stray strand of hair behind her ear. Moving his hand to her cheek, he stared intently into her eyes. Searching them. Giving her a chance to protest.

She wouldn't. She wanted him to kiss her. Her heart fluttered, and tingles rippled down her spine at the thought. He leaned closer, slowly. She parted her lips and closed her eyes, giving him permission. His lips gently brushed hers, igniting the old flame she thought had blown out.

Just as he leaned forward to deepen the kiss, his phone rang, ruining the moment. She pulled her face from his hand, stood, and started pacing next to the bed. She told herself she was glad for the interruption. Sure, in the moment and maybe even right now, she wanted him to kiss her, but she knew she was only going to get hurt again. It was best that nothing happened.

"Hello?" He answered the phone, and his face brightened at whoever was on the other end. "Jake, man, you sound much better. How are you feeling?"

When he said Jacob's name, she quit pacing. She was anxious to talk to Jacob, but it wouldn't be very nice to rip the phone from Cody's hand.

"Yeah, she's right here. It's good to hear you're feeling better. Here's Maggie." He handed the phone to her.

"Hey, big brother." She sat back down at the table

"How's my favorite little sister?" It was good to hear Jacob's voice.

"I'm your only little sister. I'm fine. How are you feeling?"

"I'm better now that I know where you are. I was worried when you didn't answer your phone or return my messages. I was afraid something happened."

"I left my cell phone at the other hotel. Along with my purse and all of my clothes."

"I see. More trouble?"

"Not really." She grimaced as she lied to him. She hated it, but he didn't need to worry about her. He had problems of his own to deal with.

"Don't lie to me, Magpie. If it weren't bad, Cody wouldn't have whisked you away without your stuff."

"You're right. Dee left a note, um, hinting at death." Her voice broke on the last word. Cody took her hand in his, holding it tightly. She smiled sadly.

Jacob groaned and there was rustling. "What are you doing?"

"I'm trying to get out of the bed. Where are you guys? I'll be there as soon as I can."

"No. Jacob, you get back in that bed. Cody is here. He's not going to let anything happen to me. I promise I will stick by his side."

Another groan. "Fine. I love you. Can I talk to Cody again?"

"I love you, too. Here's Cody." She passed him the phone.

Cody let go of her hand and took the phone. "Jake."

She couldn't hear Jacob's side of the conversation, but Cody's face hardened. "I will. I'll be sure to check in. Take care of yourself." He disconnected the call and placed the phone on the table.

"What's the matter?"

"Oh, nothing. He just threatened me with bodily harm if anything happened to you. I won't go in to detail. It was quite morbid." He smiled and winked.

"That's my big brother for you." She stood.

"He's a good one. I know you didn't get to grab your stuff last night. There's a small general store about a mile down the road. We can pick up some of the necessities. I don't know about you, but my teeth feel like sandpaper."

"And how do you suppose I pay for the necessities? With my good looks?"

"Your good looks could buy a lot with me."

She gaped at him, at a loss for words.

His face turned red. He stood and walked to the hotel door, trying to hide his embarrassment. "Seriously, I'll buy what you need, and you can pay me back when we get your purse. The first thing you should consider purchasing is a different pair of pants. While I love the ducks, some people may think you're a quack."

"You are *so* funny." Sarcasm oozed from that statement. "Okay, but you will give me the receipts so I can keep track of how much I owe you."

119

He held the door open for her, letting it close behind them. She noticed Cody positioned himself between her and the open walkway. She was protected on both sides, yet a sense of dread washed over her. She couldn't say why. Maybe it was because Cody was putting himself between her and any danger that could be lurking out there. They descended the stairs and exited the stairwell. Cody slowed and scanned the parking lot. He acted as though he suspected something was off. She followed his gaze. Satisfied, he gave her a nudge forward while he surveyed the building behind them one last time. She moved with a purpose, reached the car quickly, and opened the passenger's side door.

Her stomach roiled, and dizziness overwhelmed her at the sight of the person sitting in the passenger's seat. She slammed the door in horror and took two shaky steps backward before turning away from the car.

SIXTEEN

Maggie ran past him, not saying a word. He'd been scanning the parking lot and hadn't seen anything to cause a reaction like that. He glanced at his car; she must have seen something in it. He could see the outline of something in the passenger's seat. He needed to stop Maggie before she got hurt, and then he could assess the situation.

"Maggie, stop!" He caught up to her in three long strides, grabbed her shoulder as she made it to the stairwell, and spun her around to face him. Eyes wide with fear, she stared into space behind him, not focusing on anything, her breath coming in ragged gasps.

"Maggie." He placed his hands on her cheeks, turning her face to his. "Look at me, honey." He stared intently into her eyes, hoping for a connection to help calm her down.

She stared off in the direction of his car.

"Breathe," he said.

She continued to pant.

He brushed hair from her forehead. "Breathe with me." He took a deep breath and released it. Then he took another and released it. On the third breath, Maggie looked at him and started to breathe with him. After several calming breaths, Maggie fell into his arms and buried her face in his chest.

"She's dead." Her words were muffled, and he wasn't sure he understood her.

He pulled back slightly so he could see her eyes. "Say that again?"

"There's a dead woman in your car!" Her breathing started to pick up again.

He spun her around and pushed her toward the stairs. Knowing if what she said was true, they would be in danger standing out in the open like this. Instinctively, he unholstered his gun and disengaged the safety. Once in the covered stairwell, he made eye contact with Maggie, making sure she was focusing on him and what he was about to say.

"We are going to go back to the hotel room. I'm going to take the lead. Stay behind me and do as I say, do you understand?"

She nodded her understanding. Stepping in front of her, he led the way up the stairs, pausing at the opening to the balcony. He reached into his back pocket, pulled out his wallet, and handed it to Maggie. "Get the key card out and be ready to unlock the door." With shaking hands, she took the key card from his wallet.

He peered around the corner, checking to make sure it was clear, then led the way down the hotel balcony and stood watch over the parking lot while Maggie unlocked the door. Once she was safely in the room, he backed in, shutting the door and locking the deadbolt.

He engaged the safety on his gun, holstered it, and then lead Maggie to a chair. He pulled his phone from his pocket and dialed 911 as he walked to the hotel window. He pushed the curtain slightly to the side so he could get a good look at the parking lot.

"Nine-one-one, what's your emergency."

"This is Sheriff Cody Smith. I am at the Tumbleweed Inn on Highway 65. I have a 10-54. Civilian claims there's a dead body in a black Chevy Impala. No immediate threat noted but the area has not been secured. I have the reporting civilian in room two-oh-seven and will be going to investigate the claim."

"Ten-four, Sheriff. Units have been dispatched. I've also notified EMT and the coroner."

"Thank you."

He disconnected the call, put the phone back in his pocket, and turned to Maggie. "I need to secure the area and make sure the woman you saw in my car doesn't need medical attention."

Wrapping her arms around her midsection, she stood and paced. "Cody, she doesn't need medical attention."

Cody crossed the room and placed his hands on her shoulders to stop her pacing. "Did you recognize the woman in my car?"

"Dee."

"We don't know that Dee had anything to do with this. We won't know until we can get out there and have a look."

She shook her head. "No, Cody. It was Dee. Dee *is* the dead woman in your car!"

He stared at her like she was speaking a foreign language.

"Are you sure it was Dee? You said before that you had never seen her before that day at the sheriff's office."

"I'm sure. I may not have seen her before that day, but I *know* that is her in your car."

She shook his hands off her shoulders and resumed pacing in front of the television. Turning around, he walked back to the hotel window and moved the curtain to look out over the parking lot. He couldn't see anyone else outside. He wanted to go down, check out the scene, and start securing the perimeter, but he couldn't leave Maggie alone. Not after what she saw.

"Cody, you don't have to stay up here to babysit me. Go do your job."

"I am. My job is to protect you. There is nothing I can do for Dee now."

"I'll lock the door behind you and not open it for any one."

He looked at her and then back out the window, thinking of all the possible scenarios that could happen. Faint sirens reached his ears. Backup was almost here. He could have an officer sit with her while he checked things out.

A Prairie's Grove cruiser pulled into the parking lot and parked in front of his car. A young officer slid from the driver's seat.

"Maggie. I'm going to step outside and let the Prairie's Grove officers know what's going on. I'll be right outside the door."

She nodded solemnly.

He opened the door and closed it behind him. He pulled his badge off his belt and yelled to the officers in the parking lot. "Excuse me."

Both officers turned their attention to him, hands instinctively hovering over their service weapons.

He raised his arms, one hand showing his badge. "Cody Smith. Dale County Sheriff."

The men relaxed. "You call it in?"

"Yes. I've got the witness up here."

The other officer opened the car door with a gloved hand and bent slightly to reach into the car. He stuck his arm in and felt for a pulse. Pulling it out a few seconds later, he turned Cody's direction and shook his head. He closed the door, removed the glove, and followed the first officer.

The officers joined him on the balcony. The first officer stuck out his hand. "I'm David Jenson, and this is Garrett Masterson. Tell us what you know."

"We were headed to my car when Maggie Jones, the witness, found the body. I haven't seen it myself. Maggie says it's Dee Abrams. I can give a positive ID when I get down there. I just don't want to leave Maggie alone."

Officer Jenson took notes. "What makes her believe it's Dee Abrams?"

Cody gave them a recap of the last several days. "If one of you wants to stay up here and take Ms. Jones's statement, I can go down and positively ID the body."

"I can take her statement, and Masterson can go down with you."

Cody let Officer Jenson into the room and introduced him to Maggie. "Maggie, I'll be right downstairs. I'll be back in a few minutes."

He followed Officer Masterson down to his car. "You said this was your car?"

"Unfortunately so."

Officer Masterson put on another glove and opened the car door. Cody stepped around him and peered inside. Her body was situated in the passenger's seat. Her brown eyes were open wide, staring at something she'd never see.

"It's Dee Abrams." A pill bottle was clutched in her left hand and several bottles were scattered on the floorboard. He bent over to get a better look. There were prescriptions for antidepressants and painkillers. All prescribed to Iris Grainger.

The air swooshed out of his lungs. Was Dee responsible for Iris's death? He straightened and pointed to the pills. "This may be connected to one of my old cases. Those belong to another one of my dispatchers. She took her own life, too."

"What's that?" Officer Masterson pointed to a piece of paper in Dee's hand.

"It's probably a note. Take some pictures and let's see what it says."

Masterson walked to his cruiser and retrieved a digital camera. He took several pictures before removing the paper and unfolding it.

Six for Gold. I'm sorry.

Cody ran his hand through his hair and looked to the sky. *Lord, when I prayed for an end to this I never imagined it'd end this way.* Tires on gravel alerted him to the arrival of more people. It was the coroner's van followed by a Dale County Sheriff's cruiser.

125

"I heard it on the radio and thought I'd come see if I could help," Grainger said as he stopped next to Cody.

"It's not something we should be involved with. It's Dee."

"No." Grainger looked in the car like he didn't believe him.

"Yes. Since you're here and my car is a crime scene, can you give us a ride to the station?"

"Sure." Grainger's voice was low and raspy.

They went upstairs and waited for the officers to give them the go-ahead to leave.

Cody watched Maggie in the rearview mirror from the front passenger's seat of Grainger's cruiser. Though she said it was to give him time to talk to Grainger, he suspected she had insisted he sit up front because she needed time to think and process what she had seen this morning. There wasn't much conversation between him and Grainger, though. Cody looked back at Maggie. She sat motionless in the back seat, her head leaned back, and her eyes closed.

His mind went back to his car. The note Dee left was a blessing for him. Without it he would be sitting on the wrong side of an interrogation table.

"Cody?" Maggie's soft voice filtered through his fog of thoughts.

He turned in his seat so he could see her better. "Yes."

"What do you think Dee meant when she said *Six for Gold?*"

When he had seen the note, he knew immediately what it was referring to. Maggie didn't have any knowledge of law enforcement or their procedures and wouldn't know what it meant. He looked at Grainger, trying to figure out how to explain it to her. Grainger gave him a barely perceptible nod. Turning back to Maggie, he cleared the emotions from his throat. "People refer to police officers as blue, like men in blue. We consider our dispatchers to be invaluable. They are golden, so we refer to them as gold."

126

Her face fell, perhaps she understood why he and Grainger were saddened by Dee's death. Yes, she had done some terrible things, but that didn't lessen the pain.

"Iris was a dispatcher, too. We've lost two dispatchers in less than a year, both committing suicide," Grainger added, and his voice caught.

Maggie slumped back into her seat. The remainder of the ride into Whitehaven was filled with silence. Cody had thought Dee was working with someone, but her suicide didn't make sense if that were true. Now that she was dead, they would be able to search her house. Maybe they would find out how she knew so much about Maggie.

Dee's death created more questions than it answered. Something at the scene of Dee's suicide made him reconsider the angle that had been taken in Iris's case. Grainger pulled into the Sheriff's department and parked near the entrance, cutting into Cody's thoughts. "Grainger, I need to talk to you, so don't wander too far away."

Grainger nodded. "Sure thing. I'll be in the break room. Nice to see you again, Maggie. I wish it was under better circumstances though."

"Likewise." She waved as he turned down the hall.

Cody gestured her into his office. He closed the door, shutting out all the noise on the other side. Crossing to his desk, he grabbed her purse and belongings one of the deputies had brought back from the first hotel. She took it, her fingers brushing his, sending a spike of adrenaline through him. He crossed his arms and leaned against his desk. "I haven't told Grainger this yet, but the pill bottles Dee had belonged to Iris."

"How did she get her pills?"

"That is what I intend to find out. My hunch is that Dee may have been the one terrorizing Iris. I'm afraid we may even have to reopen Iris's case and reinvestigate her suicide." He let out an exasperated sigh and ran his hand through his disheveled hair.

"I should probably go so you can talk to Grainger. Do you have someone who can give me a ride home?"

Disappointment shot through him. He nodded and turned to open the office door, hesitated a moment, and then turned back to her. This couldn't be the end of them. She was safe now that Dee was dead, but Cody still wanted to see her. He wanted to mend the relationship he had destroyed. He didn't know if things would ever be the same, but he'd hate himself if he didn't at least try. "I know now is not the best time, but once this is all settled, I'd like to see you again. I mean, outside of the role of sheriff."

"I—I don't think that's a good idea, Cody." She walked around him, opened the door, and stepped into the hall without saying another word.

His shoulders sank. She'd forgiven him, and he'd thought she was warming up to the possibility of them. Was she still harboring insecurities because of him? Once everything was cleared with Dee, he planned to talk with her. He couldn't let her keep believing the lies she'd been telling herself.

"Deputy Minton," he called to his deputy sitting at the information desk, "could you please take Ms. Jones home?"

"Yes, sir." Deputy Minton led the way out the front door, Maggie following. She didn't bother saying good-bye.

He stood in the doorway of his office watching Maggie's retreating figure. Her dismissal was a blow he hadn't been prepared for.

"Hey, boss, you wanted to talk?" Grainger stood next to Cody, following his gaze. "How are things going mending that relationship?" Grainger had been Cody's closest friend since the summer he'd ended things with Maggie and subsequently distanced himself from Jake. Grainger knew they had dated. As a matter of fact, half the town probably knew.

128

One night, about a year and half ago, he and Grainger were consoling Deputy Minton at the diner. Mrs. Minton had left him, and Cody was trying to encourage him to fight for his wife, not to give up like he had done with Maggie. The diner was crowded so he had to speak loudly, and anyone there could have heard their conversation.

"I don't want to talk about it."

"That bad, huh?"

"I thought telling her the truth would at least be a step in the right direction. But she's not interested."

"Man, I'm sorry." Grainger clapped his hand on Cody's back. "At least she's safe now. Give her some time to sort through the last couple of days."

"Speaking of that, step into my office. We need to talk."

Grainger's face darkened. "Why do I get the feeling I'm not going to like this?"

Cody followed him into the office and shut the door. "Have a seat." Cody took his chair behind the desk while Grainger took one that faced the desk.

"What's this about, Sheriff?" Grainger adjusted his utility belt to better fit the chair.

"How well did Iris know Dee?"

Grainger's brows knitted together as he tilted his head to the side. "They were coworkers. You know that. But I don't think they did much outside of work. Why?"

"I'm going to be completely honest with you, and I hope you'll do the same." Cody didn't want to open old wounds. He'd watch his reactions to the conversation before he'd make a decision about removing him from the case.

"I always am."

"We found prescription bottles around Dee's body. They were all prescribed to Iris."

Grainger's eyes widened, and he blew out a heavy sigh. "Whoa. Are you thinking Dee was Iris's stalker?"

"I don't know for certain, but it's definitely an avenue that needs exploring now."

Grainger leaned farther back in the chair and hung his head back, staring at the ceiling. He sat motionless for a minute. Cody was about to say something when he sat up. "Now what?"

"Now we go through Iris's case again and see if we can connect Dee to anything. We also need to find out how Dee got Iris's prescriptions. What did you do with them when you cleaned out her house?"

"I took them to the pharmacy and turned them in."

Cody made a mental note to call the pharmacy when they were open and ask what the process would have been after they were turned over. "Do you think you can go through Iris's file with me? If you need to take some time, it's perfectly understandable."

Grainger straightened. "No. I'm fine to continue."

Cody had been watching him the entire time. His face had portrayed the sadness he undoubtedly felt. "Okay. I'll grab the file and meet you in the conference room."

They spent the better part of the next two hours going over the things that had happened to Iris, trying to see if there was any clue that Dee could have been the stalker and found nothing.

SEVENTEEN

Deputy Minton hadn't only dropped Maggie off at the house, he had done a walk through before he left. He said that Dee may be dead and the threat gone but, that didn't mean she hadn't left any surprises. After he'd left, she took a long, hot shower, washing away the grime from the past few days, literally at least. Figuratively, it was going to take a lot longer for her to feel clean.

She dug her phone out of her purse, hoping to call and check on Jacob. As her recent luck would have it, her battery was dead. She connected it to the charger and used the house phone.

"Hello?"

"Hey, Jacob. How are you feeling?" She sat on the couch, drawing her knees up.

"I'm going crazy. I can't wait to get out of this hospital."

She laughed. Jacob had never liked being cooped up. "Any idea when you'll get to go home?"

"Actually, yes. They are working on the discharge paperwork now."

"That's great. I'll come get you." It would give her something to do besides sit in the big, old house by herself.

"No. You need to stay with Cody. I'll find a ride home."

"It's okay now. We found Dee's body this morning. I'm safe." She slid her shoes on.

"We? What do you mean *we*?" His voice rose an octave.

She filled him in on everything that had happened since their last phone call.

"That's good. Well, not that she's dead but that you're safe."

"Yes, it is. Now, I can actually breathe. And I can focus on the house. Except tonight, I'm going to come pick you up and give you a ride home."

"Sounds good to me."

She hung up, gathered her things, drove to the hospital, and waited for his release. After he'd signed all the discharge paperwork, she drove them to his house, where he lay on the couch, protesting. Self-sufficiency was apparently a family trait and being cared for made Jacob ornery. "I'm not helpless, you know."

"No, but it's the least I can do. If it wasn't for me, you wouldn't have been hurt."

Before he had a chance to argue, the doorbell rang, and she jumped up to answered it. She paid the deliveryman and took the pizza to the living room, setting it on the coffee table in front of Jacob. She'd ordered pizza when she had gotten him home because she didn't want him cooking and truthfully, she didn't feel like cooking, either. She brought him a plate and he sat up to eat. She busied herself by taking care of his laundry and making sure he had everything he needed. Keeping busy was her way of avoiding going back to her father's house.

Sure, Dee was dead, and Maggie could go on with her life. She didn't have to be afraid of what sick trick would come next or if she would get hurt. But going on with her life meant going through her father's things and all the memories they would conjure. It also meant leaving Whitehaven... and Cody.

Looking around the house, she still saw touches of her sister-in-law throughout the home. For the millionth time, she wondered how Jacob had gotten through each day after Caroline's car accident. Her gruff, macho brother had been head-over-heels in love with his sweet wife, and her death had devastated him. She got the impression that he worked too much and kept to himself, and he'd never been one to talk about his feelings. But he'd figured out a way to continue on.

Their little family seemed plagued by loss, and now she and Jacob were both alone. Something had changed in him though—over the past three months, every time they ended a phone conversation, he'd told her that he loved her. It was almost as if he had decided that he didn't want to leave the important things unsaid. She thought again of Cody. How different would their lives have been if they had the chance to go back and really say what was in their hearts. There was no changing the past, but what would it mean for them now if they just said what they felt? If she told him how *she* felt? Something soft hit the side of her head, jarring her back to reality.

"What's going on in that little brain of yours?" Jacob teased as he threw another pillow at her. Before it could hit her, she caught it and squeezed it to her chest.

"I know these are called throw pillows, but it's not so you can throw them at people." She hugged it and then as quickly as she could, she launched it at his head, hoping to catch him off guard. He dodged it at the last second and it sailed behind the couch.

"You throw like a girl." He laughed. "Seriously, Mags, you don't have to stay here and coddle me. I know you blame yourself for what happened, but it is not your fault."

He stood and grimaced as he straightened. Guilt overwhelmed her as he slowly started walking toward the end of the couch. *Is it time for his medicine?*

She jumped up and met him at the end of the couch before he could turn and go down the hall to the kitchen. "What do you need? I can get it for you."

He grabbed her in a hug and squeezed until she was sure she was going to break in half. "Thank God you are okay. I'm so thankful Cody was around to keep you safe."

133

"Yes. Cody. My hero." Her voice was flat. He actually was her hero, but she didn't want to talk about him, especially with Jacob.

"What's that about?"

She pulled away and wrapped her arms around her midsection. "Nothing. I don't want to talk about it."

"Fine." He pushed past her, circling behind the couch.

"Jacob Anthony Jones, you sit right back down. Whatever you need, I can get it for you."

He bent over, picked up the errant pillow, and tossed it at her again.

"Number one, your teacher voice doesn't work with me. Number two, I need to use the bathroom, and I don't think that's something you want to help with. And number three, we're talking when I get back." He ambled to the bathroom.

She grabbed a slice of pizza and bit into it. She didn't want to talk to Jacob about what was going on. He didn't need to worry about her; he needed to focus on getting better. Plus, she just really didn't want to talk with him about Cody.

Jacob came back into the room and lowered himself on the couch. "Tell me what's going on. Is it the stalker situation or something else? Do Cody and I need to kick some butt?"

She laughed at the image of Cody trying to beat himself up. "No. There's no need to beat anyone up. Dee is gone, so I don't have to worry about that craziness anymore. It's just... being back home is hard. Being back in Whitehaven is bringing up old memories and being around Cody, well, that's another story."

"Come sit." He patted the couch next to him. As soon as she sat down, he pulled her into the crook of his arm and gave her a noogie. She squealed and batted at him, careful not to actually hit him. She pulled herself out of his hold, grabbed a throw pillow, and scooted over, out of his reach. She leaned her back against the arm of the couch and brought her knees to her chest, placing the pillow on top and resting her chin on it.

"I know it's hard, especially being at the house. I'm sure you see mom and dad everywhere. I know I do when I'm there. You could stay here if you'd like."

Grief crawled from her chest and escaped through the tears that fell from her eyes. "It's more than that. I need to be at the house and working on it."

"Want to talk about it?"

"Not really. It might make me feel better, though."

He turned his body to her, resting his arm against the back of the couch.

"You remember the summer before I left for college?"

He nodded.

"Well, I was seeing someone, and he dumped me a week before I left. I was pretty wrecked over it. Being back is not only bringing up memories of mom and dad but of him, too."

"I knew it. I told Cody I thought you were seeing someone. I just couldn't figure out who it was. It's been six years, but I can still kick his butt for hurting you. Just give me a name."

She shook her head and gave him a weak smile. "What is it with you and kicking butts?"

He shrugged.

"There's no need for any bodily harm. He's apologized. Those old memories are bringing up old feelings. I think he wants to try again... Part of me wants to, too." She gazed around Jacob's living room, looking at the pictures on the mantle. His graduation. Caroline on their wedding day. Jacob and Cody as teenagers.

"Why don't you give it a try?"

"What?" She looked at him quizzically.

"If he wants to try and you want to try, then why not try?"

"I don't want to try and get hurt again." She looked back at the picture of Caroline. She looked so happy. Maggie wanted a happiness like that.

"I can understand. Close your eyes."

135

"Why?" She frowned.

"Just do it."

"Fine." She closed her eyes and waited for him to punch her or pull her hair like he used to do when they were kids.

"Picture the man you dated."

"Okay." She pictured Cody. First, she saw him as the young teenager she dated. Then she envisioned the man he was today.

"You see him?" Jacob's voice was a tad quieter than before.

"Yes." She nodded.

"Okay. How do you feel?"

"I feel foolish."

This time, he did punch her, softly on the arm. "Come on. When you see him standing there, what do you feel? What do you remember?"

What did she feel when she pictured him? Warmth started in her chest and spread throughout her body. The feelings she had for Cody washed over her. She felt loved. Cherished. Happy. "I feel like I'm home."

"Okay. So, isn't it worth trying to get back there? It may not happen, but if you don't try you won't know. You can't do something because you're afraid to get hurt."

"I suppose you're right."

"Okay. Here's a better explanation. If I were suddenly transported back to the day I met Caroline and I had the knowledge of what our future would hold, I wouldn't change a thing. Loving her and being loved by her was one of the greatest things I've ever experienced. Losing her was... unbearable, but it could never hurt enough to erase what we had. Love is so much stronger than that pain."

"How'd you get so smart?"

"Wisdom comes with age." He assumed an exaggeratedly enlightened expression, reached over and took the pillow from under her chin, then smacked her with it. He smiled. "Now, who's the lucky guy?"

She tried to steal the pillow but was unsuccessful. "Uh, no. That's for me to know. I need to get back to the house. I have a lot to think about." She gave Jacob a hug. "Thanks, big brother. Call me if you need anything."

"I'm not an invalid, but I will call. The offer still stands, you're welcome to stay here."

She slipped her feet into her shoes and hooked her purse on her shoulder. "No. I tend to clean while I think. Maybe I'll get the house done tonight."

"Good luck."

She shut the door behind her and headed to the truck.

* * * *

A noise had seeped into Maggie's dream, stirring her awake. She didn't know what it was or where it had come from, but she didn't hear anything now. The clock on her nightstand read 2:57 a.m. She closed her eyes and willed herself to go back to sleep. It had only been an hour since she went to bed, but her brain wouldn't allow it. She thought about everything that still needed to be done. Part of her wanted to hire an auctioneer and sell it all off. Jacob had already claimed what he wanted of their parent's belongings, and he didn't want anything else. What was the point in boxing it all up and letting it gather dust?

Another noise drifted into her bedroom, sounding like it came from downstairs. Sitting up, she slipped her feet into her duck slippers and padded down the hallway to the stairs. The house was so old it was probably a shutter flapping in the wind.

As she neared the bottom of the stairs, she saw a soft glow coming from the living room. *Didn't I turn off all the lights before going to bed?* She had been so tired after coming home and packing and cleaning the kitchen and Jacob's old room.

She descended the last step and turned to the living room, coming to an abrupt halt. Dee's face stared back at her from the television screen.

She froze at the base of the stairs, staring at a video of Dee sitting in what appeared to be a car. She needed to call for help. No, she needed to run, but her feet were glued to the floor. Dee's voice played over the speakers.

"Oooh, the sheriff's car is comfy. We can just take some pictures to let them know how much we're enjoying it." Dee was laughing, looking at someone off camera. "I'll text them to her and remind her that we can find her anywhere."

Dee lifted a phone, took a few of the view from out the car windshield, then started taking photos of herself. She took a few smiling photos and then a photo blowing kisses to the camera. "I love it. They're up there sleeping. They don't even know we're down here. I can't wait to see the look on their faces." She giggled, vicious delight in her eyes. Her expression turned adoring as she said, "I love you," and blew a kiss to whoever was off camera.

"Hey, stop, what is that?" Panic laced her voice. "What are you doing?" She started to get out of the car, but a gloved hand pushed her back in and then another gloved hand entered the frame and pushed a needle into Dee's neck.

"What was in that? You didn't say anything…" Dee's words slurred, and her eyes drooped. After a moment, her head rolled back to the headrest. The gloved hand placed two fingers on her neck, checking for a pulse. He turned her head toward the door and opened her eyes so she would be staring at whoever opened the door. A small piece of paper was placed in front of the camera. *Seven for a Secret Never to be Told.* Then the gloved hand covered the camera that must have been positioned on the dashboard.

Maggie couldn't move, her body was paralyzed with fear. Dee hadn't killed herself. Someone had murdered her. There was a second person. *And they are in the house!*

She turned and ran up the stairs, but her feet wouldn't cooperate. She tripped, banging her shin on the edge of one of the stairs, sending shooting pain down her leg. She stood and continued clumsily climbing the stairs. She ran to her bedroom, shut the door, and moved a chair to position the back under the doorknob. Hopefully that would be enough to keep her intruder out. She ran to the nightstand and grabbed her cell phone from where she had left it charging.

She dialed Cody's number, her fingers shaking so badly she had to dial twice before she got it right.

Pick up. Please pick up.

EIGHTEEN

The ringing phone was somewhere to his right. He threw his hand in the direction of the sound and felt around haplessly on the nightstand. He opened his eyes and focused on the sliver of light indicating the incoming call. After swiping the screen, he put the phone to his ear. "Sheriff Smith here." His greeting was met by silence. "Hello? Who is it?"

There was a shuffling noise on the other end and stifled a sob. He pulled the phone away from his ear, squinting against the bright light and checked the caller ID.

Maggie.

Why was she calling him in the middle of the night, or morning actually? She wouldn't be calling him unless it was important. "What's wrong?"

"Cody." He could hear her ragged breathing. "Dee didn't kill herself."

His tired brain stumbled over her words. "The coroner thinks it's a suicide. We won't know for sure until after the autopsy, but I hope you're not worrying over this. Maggie, it was—"

"No, listen to me, Cody. Dee didn't kill herself, someone else did. And they filmed it."

"What? How do—?"

"Someone broke into the house and put it in the DVD player." She was starting to gasp for air. "They could still be here."

He jumped out of bed and pulled on a shirt and his tennis shoes. It was a good thing he had been too tired to undress completely before he fell asleep. "I'm on my way. Stay on the line with me, okay?"

He grabbed his keys and gun holster before tearing out the front door.

"Y-yes." She hiccupped.

"Where are you? Are you somewhere safe?"

"I've locked myself in my room, and I shoved a chair under the door knob."

He slung the truck door open, jumped in, started the engine, and gunned it out of the drive. "I'll be there in ten minutes." The drive would normally take twenty-five minutes but with it being this early in the morning there wouldn't be any traffic, and he had no intention of following the speed limit. In the meantime, he needed to make sure she was absolutely safe. "Do you hear anything to let you know the intruder might still be there?"

The silence on her end of the line seemed to go on forever.

"Maggie?"

"I'm here, I don't hear anything."

"Good, do you still have your father's gun?

"Uh huh."

"I want you to get it and keep it by you. If anyone forces their way through that door, you shoot, okay?"

He heard shuffling on her side of the line as he assumed she was getting the gun. His foot stomped the accelerator, pushing the odometer higher. He needed to get to Maggie before someone else did.

God, keep her safe. I don't know what I will do if I lose her.

He needed to alert his deputies, but he was in a rental that didn't have a police radio. He couldn't bring himself to hang up on her to sever the connection. He would keep her on the line, that way he would know if something happened. He could hear her murmuring prayers, and he prayed along with her.

The trip to Maggie's house was agonizing. He took the turn on her drive so fast that the rear tires skidded, causing the rear end to kick sideways. He let off the accelerator before he lost control. Once the car straightened, he gunned it again and raced up her drive. He skidded to a stop in front of the porch steps.

"Maggie, I'm here. I'm going to hang up. Do not open that door until you hear my voice on the other side."

"Okay," she squeaked.

He threw his cell phone in the seat, pulled his gun from the holster, and charged up the porch steps. He tried the front door, but it was locked. He took a step back and did a couple well-placed kicks, shattering the old wood door frame, setting off the alarm and allowing him access.

He slowly entered the living room and looked around. Dee's face was frozen on the television screen. He cleared the rest of the room and then quickly cleared the downstairs, too. He took the stairs one at a time and cleared each bedroom before coming to the room he knew was Maggie's. He slid the safety in place and tucked his gun in its holster.

He knocked on the door. "Maggie, it's Cody. You can open up now."

Her footsteps quickly crossed the room and the chair scraped across the floor as she removed it from the doorknob. She flung the door open and threw her arms around him. She squeezed like she would never let go. He buried his face into her tangled hair as he clutched her to his chest. Pulling back slightly, he looked at her and whispered, "Thank God, you're safe."

Tendrils of hair covered her face. He smoothed them away so he could stare into her beautiful eyes. He rested his hand on her cheek and before he could stop himself, he lowered his head and gently brought his lips to hers.

Her lips were as soft as he remembered. As he started to pull away, she threaded her hand through his hair and pulled him back to her. The passion with which she kissed him awoke the feelings that had laid dormant since that night long ago.

He let his hand fall from her face and slide down her arm, wrapping behind her and pulling her closer. She slowly slid her hand down his cheek and rested it on his chest, leaving a trail of fire in its wake. Could she feel his heart racing? Slowly, the kiss ended, and he rested his forehead against hers. She closed her eyes, and her breath came in small gasps.

He wanted to stay like this forever, but this was not the time or place. Right now, he needed to concentrate on keeping her safe. He stepped back, immediately missing her presence.

He rubbed the tension from the back of his neck. "I'm sorry, Magpie, we need to go. But uh, first, can we turn off the alarm?"

"Oh. Yeah." Her bright eyes dulled, and she walked passed him and down the stairs. He followed. She quickly disarmed the alarm and ran back up to her room. He thought he saw a tear slide down her cheek as she blew past him.

He grabbed the cordless phone and called the incident in. She reappeared at the top of the stairs, a small overnight bag in one hand and a dejected expression on her face.

"Come on, honey. Let's get out of here."

She descended the stairs. "Where are we going to go now? Where are we going to hide while we wait for the next line of the stupid nursery rhyme?"

"Magpie, I know that you're frustrated and scared. I don't blame you but—"

"You *don't* know what I am feeling right now."

"You're right. I don't, but I can assume. I've got my best deputies working on this."

He took her hand and led her to the front door, using their connected hands to direct her behind him. They walked quickly to his truck.

Every muscle in his body was on alert. He was watching their surroundings as they walked. He opened the door for Maggie and closed it behind her after she climbed in. Walking around to the driver's side he climbed in, started the truck, and took off, not bothering to buckle his seatbelt until the truck was in motion.

He glanced at her as they barreled down the road. She sat in the passenger's seat of his truck, tracing her lips with her fingers. Did they still tingle like his?

"Tell me about the video."

She told him about the noise waking her up and then the walk downstairs to find the video playing on her television screen. "After he felt for a pulse, he turned her head to stare at the door. He purposely opened her eyes, too, like he knew I'd be the one to open the door. Then a piece of paper was held up that read *Seven for a Secret Never to be Told.*" She punched her leg with her fist. "What have I done? Who is doing this to me and why? Lord, I don't understand."

He reached over and grabbed her hand. "I don't know the answer to those questions. But I do know I will not stop looking for him."

She yanked her hand from his, throwing her hands in the air in exasperation. "Yeah, but do you actually think you'll ever find him? He doesn't leave evidence. Every time I hide, he finds me. It feels *hopeless*. I just want this to be over. I want to pack up my dad's stuff, and I want to go home and never think about Whitehaven again."

He put his hand back on the steering wheel. Her words stung. Did she really want to leave or was she just frustrated with her situation? The way she'd kissed him... ^Pit had been like she was trying to pack the last six years into one kiss. All he could rationally discuss was the threat.

"I pray that I do find him, and fast. First Iris and now you. Two seemingly different women. It really seems like he has picked his targets at random, but there's got to be a connection."

145

Maggie didn't know Iris. The Grainger family had moved to town after she had already left for college. She'd had no connection with this town since she left, except when she came home to visit her father, which was why he couldn't figure out who was after her.

Cody slowed the truck and flipped on the turn signal, pulling into the Dale County Sheriff's parking lot.

"Dee's death is now officially a homicide. There are things I need to do now that can't wait for later. There's a small room where you can rest. Then we can go to my house where you can get proper sleep." She started to protest, but he interrupted her with a raised hand. "I know you don't want to stay with me, but at this point we don't have a choice."

"Okay." She followed him into the station. He led her down a hallway to a sparsely furnished office. An old, rickety cot was pushed up against the wall on the right. Directly across from it was a small desk and chair.

"We call this the crash room. We use it when there's an emergency situation and all hands are on deck. It's mostly used during a missing persons case, which we haven't had in a long time. Deputies can come in here and catch a few winks after an arduous search. I've slept on it myself a time or two. It's not the most comfortable bed in the world, but it will do."

"I'm not sure I'm going to be able to sleep but I'll stay in here and out of your way."

"We've got a break room with a couple vending machines and some outdated magazines, or you can sit in my office while I work."

"I don't want to be in the way. I'll sit in the break room."

"Okay, right this way."

After getting Maggie settled in the break room, he called Deputy Bennet to check on the progress of securing Maggie's house. Then he called Deputy Minton to do a complete work up of the scene. While all deputies had basic crime scene gear in their patrol vehicles, Minton was the official crime scene investigator. He had several hours of training every year with outside agencies, and he was always taking classes or reading the newest forensic discoveries. Now that their stalking and suicide case was now a murder investigation, Minton would be the only deputy to work any related crime scenes.

The time on the computer showed a quarter to five. It was still too early to call the pharmacy about the disposal of Iris's prescriptions. At this point, he wasn't even sure that was what killed Dee. Maggie said the video clearly showed Dee being stabbed with a syringe. It would still be a while before the toxicology report came back. He made a note to call the medical examiner to see if there had been any evidence that might lead them to a certain class of drugs.

With nothing left for him to do at the moment, Cody turned off the desk lamp and went to find Maggie. She was exactly where he had left her, sitting at the table. She was busy writing on what appeared to be a paper towel she'd pulled from the dispenser. As he stepped closer, he noticed several other scribbled-on paper towels.

"You know you could have asked for some paper?"

She jumped at the sound of his voice. "I didn't want to bother anyone. Have a seat."

He pulled a chair over and sat close enough to read what she was writing.

"What is this?"

"I've been thinking long and hard about all of this. But first, I want to apologize. What I said earlier was out of line. It's not your fault at all. I was just lashing out." She dipped her chin, avoiding his eyes.

"It's okay. I forgive you." He raised her chin. "This is an extremely stressful situation for you. Now, about the notes?" He nodded at the paper towel.

"Right." She nodded, returning her attention to her notes. "I am absolutely positive I have never seen Dee before I met her here. If

147

I've never met her, then whoever she is, uh, was working with has to be the one that has the connection with me. Up until Dee's death, everything had been focused on me."

She handed him the stack of paper towels. The one on top had *one for sorrow* written across the top and details about the incident listed underneath it. Each additional paper towel represented the other lines of the nursery rhyme.

He was impressed with her organizational skills and the clarity with which she had documented every incident with excruciating detail. He looked at each individual paper towel.

Not only did she list the line and its corresponding act, but she also jotted down what she thought the line could mean.

One for sorrow.

Bean bag shot at Cody and me.

One shot. Sorrow—distress.

Two for joy.

Mom and dad's rings stolen.

Two—two rings. Joy—marriage/weddings are joyous occasions.

A large yawn erupted from Maggie, distorting her facial features. She needed to get some rest.

"You did a good job. It's too early for me to start making some of the phone calls that I need to make, so why don't we go to my house? That way you can get some rest and I can go over these notes."

When the argument he was expecting didn't occur, he stood and gathered Maggie's notes, tucking them in his pocket so he could examine them later.

NINETEEN

The ride from the sheriff's station to Cody's house took five minutes. Maggie grabbed her bag from the floorboard and exited the truck. Cody unlocked the front door and turned on the light as he stepped in.

The room was modestly decorated. There was a black couch and loveseat in an L shape, with an end table at the corner, and a matching entertainment center boasting a large television. The only thing hanging on the walls were the speakers to his surround sound system. It was definitely a bachelor pad.

She shut the door behind her and set her bag on the floor, bringing her hand to her mouth to cover the yawn that was forcing its way out.

"I'll show you to the guest room." He picked up her bag and led the way down a hall on the opposite side of the living room. Walking into the first room on the right, he turned the light on, illuminating a room that doubled as an office. This area was as sparse as the living room. A cheap metal desk containing a desktop computer lined one wall. A full-size bed was pushed into the corner. The bedspread was light blue with white flowers. She couldn't help but laugh at the bedding choice.

"What's so funny?" He simulated a shocked expression.

"Nothing. It's not what I pictured your decorating style would include, that's all."

"Laugh all you want. It may be dainty, but it's comfortable. It was my grandmother's. My mom left it when she stayed here last."

Maggie's heart ached as she remembered him talking about his grandmother being a big part of his life. When she died, all he had left was his mother, and most of the time she hadn't been home. That's when his behavior had taken a nosedive. He'd had a rough childhood—his father left when he was very young, and his mother had been there physically but not emotionally.

"I'm sorry. How is your mom?"

"Don't be. She's sober going on three years now."

"That's good to hear."

"Now, get some rest. We'll talk when you wake up." He set her bag on the bed and left the room, closing the door on his way out.

She put the bag on the floor, kicked off her shoes, and climbed under the covers. The bed was soft and warm, and she was exhausted, yet still she tossed and turned. Her mind wouldn't stop replaying the video of Dee's death. She tried thinking of other things, like the kiss she and Cody had shared. He'd said he wanted to see her again. And, after her talk with Jacob, she was willing to try again.

Tonight, he'd kissed her like she meant the world to him. Like he was making up for the kisses he'd missed since he'd foolishly listened to her brother. Then almost immediately, he said he was sorry. He'd regretted kissing her in the midst of the chaos. Ultimately, Cody was still putting her off, choosing a "safer" option *for* her.

She knew if she let her guard down, Cody would break her heart again. His comfort and protection was what she wanted most at the moment, but she could feel herself diving headfirst right back into all of her old emotions. Every moment longer she spent in his company was likely to result in heartbreak. Again. She felt so close to tears. The fear and worry had made her brittle - emotionally vulnerable. His kiss and subsequent reaction almost broke her. If she wasn't careful, she would throw herself into his arms, her heart for the taking. She had to keep her distance.

150

Dwelling on it wouldn't do any good. She'd drown her sorrows in the cleanup of the house. There was so much that needed to be done before they could sell it. She tried to calm herself, methodically going over her to-do list in her mind. Every room needed painting, as did the outside. The video of Dee popped back in the forefront of her thoughts. No matter how hard she tried, she couldn't get her brain to shut off.

It was no use, she wasn't going to sleep anytime soon. She got out of bed and opened the door. The lights in the front of the house were still blazing. She walked down the hall and found Cody sitting on the couch, his Bible in his hands.

"Couldn't sleep?" he asked as he closed the Bible.

"No, too much on my mind. May I have something to drink?"

"Yes. Let me show you where everything is." He set his Bible on the coffee table and led the way to the kitchen.

The kitchen had a small, connected breakfast nook containing a matching table and chairs. Black canisters lined a counter top. They matched the black appliances. His refrigerator had a calendar stuck to it, along with some various papers. Bills, maybe.

Pulling two glasses from the cabinet, he gestured to the refrigerator. "I have some sweet tea and orange juice. I'd stay away from the milk. It might be past its due date."

She loved his tea and hoped he still made it the same way. He'd spent so much time eating dinner at their house growing up, her mother treated him as one of her own. While she and Jacob were charged with setting the table, Cody was given the job of making tea. He always added too much sugar. She loved it syrupy sweet. On the days Cody wasn't around, momma made the tea, and she never used as much sugar.

She took a sip of the tea she'd poured herself and let out a small sigh as her taste buds danced in the sweet liquid. "I love your tea."

Cody sat down across from her and chuckled. "I couldn't tell."

She put her cup down on the table and ran her finger around the mouth of it. "Cody, I don't understand this. I don't know what I've done to cause all of this. We don't even know who it is! You know, in the beginning it was little scary things but now someone is dead. Not just dead but murdered. All because of me."

"You can't blame yourself for this. It is not your fault. Whoever is doing this is at fault, they have only fixated their sick game on you."

"Logically, I know that, but I still can't escape the guilt."

"Could we pray?"

"I'd like that." She closed her eyes and started saying a silent prayer.

"Dear Lord, thank You again for this day. Thank You for keeping Maggie safe. I pray that You'll continue to keep her safe and give her peace in knowing that this is not her fault. Comfort her in this difficult time. I pray for Your guidance in finding the person at fault. Amen."

"Thank you." They sat in companionable silence and sipped their tea.

"Jacob went home last night," Maggie volunteered, breaking the silence.

"That's great. How's he feeling?"

"He's sore but okay. We talked for a little while last night... He still doesn't know about us."

He looked in to his tea glass, avoiding her gaze. "I never said anything. After you left, Jake and I kind of went our separate ways. We didn't stop being friends exactly. But he had his Army life. I went into law enforcement and had my life. He married Caroline and they had their life together. After Caroline's death, he poured himself into his work and was hardly home. And being Sheriff has kept me busy."

"Are you sure it wasn't because you were afraid he'd kick your butt for hurting his little sister?" She took a drink of her tea and arched her eyebrows.

"Whatever! I always won our tussles." Laugh lines creased his face.

"Sure. Admit it, you were scared," she teased.

The laugh lines disappeared, and his face hardened. "I was honestly waiting for him to come beat down my door that first week. Then he left, and you left a couple days after. I'm surprised you didn't tell him."

"No, I didn't tell him. He actually still doesn't know. He was going back to the Army, and he'd recently started dating a girl. He always worried too much about me and he didn't need to be weighed down with my baggage. But that's all in the past. Since we're stuck with each other, tell me what made you choose law enforcement."

"That's an easy one. Remember right before we started dating I had been in some trouble?"

She nodded, taking a drink of her tea.

"Sheriff Rogers kept in touch with me and mentored me. After you left, the guys I had gotten into trouble with were all arrested. Most of them are now serving some hefty jail time. A lot of people saved me from winding up in there with them. Jesus saved my soul, you saved my heart, and Sheriff Rogers saved my life. I wanted to do that. I wanted to help others. I signed up for the police academy the week after you left. What about you? An elementary school librarian, huh?"

Her cheeks started to heat. "Yeah. That was only meant to be a stepping stone in my career, but I sort of fell in love with helping kids. Nothing beats the look on a child's face when they finally understand something they've been struggling with for a long time."

"What about your writing?"

"I still write. I had some things published in magazines and anthologies, but I haven't submitted anything in a long time." Her eyes were heavy with sleep, and a yawn forced its way from her mouth.

"You should go lie back down and get some rest."

"I think I'll try again. Here's hoping it's successful this time. Goodnight, Cody."

"Goodnight, Maggie."

TWENTY

Cody made sure all the windows around the house were locked. He always kept them latched, but he wasn't going to take anything for granted. Satisfied that the house was secure, he went back to the couch and pulled Maggie's notes from his pocket. He looked at every word, staying vigilant for any noise out of the ordinary.

When he began to get drowsy, he started a pot of coffee, grabbed the notes, a notebook and a pen and sat at the kitchen table, making his own notes. He listed all the lines from the rhyme and each act that accompanied them. Maggie was right, everything was centered around her except Dee's murder.

One for sorrow. Maggie was standing on her father's porch, in the middle of nowhere, twenty minutes outside of town, when the beanbag was shot.

Two for joy. Her parents' rings had been stolen from the house and delivered to her.

Three for a girl. Her best friend's car was vandalized.

Four for a boy. Her brother was attacked.

Five for silver. Her hotel room was vandalized and a veiled threat left on her birthday.

Six for gold. Dee was dead.

Seven for a secret never to be told. Dee's death was revealed as a homicide.

Maybe if they could get one step ahead of this guy, they could stop him. He grabbed his laptop off the kitchen counter where he had left it yesterday afternoon. Booting up the search engine, he began researching the rhyme. There were several different versions of the rhyme and a lot of them ended with the number seven. There were, of course, other versions that went as high as fourteen. Cody found a rhyme that he thought could be the one their guy was using. If that was so, there would be a number eight, *for a wish*.

How could someone do something dastardly with a wish?

He refilled his coffee cup and did another walk through of the house. He stopped outside the guest room and listened for anything out of sorts. Satisfied Maggie was sleeping soundly, he went back to the living room. He pulled the Bible from the end table and turned to Psalms.

* * * *

Shuffling seeped into his subconscious and startled him awake. He was on his feet, with his hand resting on the butt of the gun on his hip when Maggie emerged from the hallway. He relaxed, taking his hand away from the gun.

He must have dozed off because the sun was streaming through the front window blinds, casting stripes of golden sun on the floor. He rubbed the sleep from his eyes and ran his hand through his rumpled hair. "Sleep well?"

"Not really." She took a seat on his couch. "You?"

"Some." He walked to the window and looked out on to the front yard. He didn't see anything out of the ordinary. He turned back to Maggie and gestured her to the kitchen. "Would you like something to eat? I've got some cereal, but the milk is definitely bad. Found that out when I tried to add some to my coffee this morning. I might have some toaster pastries. Want one? Unless you want dry cereal."

"I haven't had a toaster pastry in ages. What are you, nine?"

"Hey, don't knock the tarts."

He followed her into the kitchen, grabbed the box from the pantry, and offered them to her. After she took one, he grabbed one for himself and put the box back in the pantry.

"I'll be right back." He put his toaster pastry on the table, walked through the house, and went outside to check the perimeter. He was probably being ridiculous, but he couldn't be too careful. Everything was in order. He returned to the kitchen. "I did some research while you were sleeping, and I think I might know what the next line is. 'Eight for a wish.' Can you think of anything that he could use for that line?"

She took a bite from the toaster pastry. "I have wishes—who doesn't—but I can't think of anything that he could use."

"Why don't you humor me and tell me some of them."

"Okay." She put down her food. "One of my big wishes is to get kids reading more. In today's day and age, it seems like no one reads anymore. Everyone is consumed with electronic devices. Reading is good for the brain, and believe it or not, you learn while you read, even if you're reading for enjoyment."

"You've always been a bookwork. Remember that year you asked everyone to buy you books for your birthday?" He opened the shiny package containing his breakfast.

"That was every year." She chuckled.

"True." He nodded. "Back to the kids, how would you accomplish that?"

"Reading contests. Not like who can read the best but more like an achievement type contest. I do a small contest where they're rewarded for reading." She took another bite. "What I'd really like to do is pick one book a month for each age group and have a month-long party based on it. Arts and crafts. Costume parties. Fun recipes. The whole shebang. Unfortunately, there's not enough funding."

She had always been creative. He had no doubt she'd make her program a huge success.

"I've also got the kids I tutor. I'd love to have more resources to help them. Not every child learns the same way. It'd be great to have things that help me cater to each learning type."

Her eyes were alight while she talked about helping others. He noticed she hadn't list any personal wishes. He thought it would be safe to rule out any of those other things. Everything that had happened involving Maggie had been personal to her and had happened here in Whitehaven, not in Houston.

"What about personal wishes?" he prodded, hoping she would open up a little.

"Well, I'd like to be a published author someday. Of course, there's the typical girl wishes, you know, marriage and kids." She toyed with the plastic package from her breakfast.

He had wanted those things, too. He'd wanted them with Maggie and had even been prepared for the next stage in their relationship. He had the ring to prove it, still in the velvet box from the jeweler. He hadn't been able to part with it, even after all these years. It was tucked away in a drawer in his bedroom.

"I can't think of anything that he could use. I really can't, unless maybe it has something to do with my dad's stuff."

Maybe there wasn't anything to the typical wishes of marriage and kids, but she had mentioned her writing. To destroy everything that someone had worked hard on could be devastating to that person. "Where do you keep the things that you write?"

"Well, I used to have it saved on my laptop. I'd back it up to a thumb drive every couple of months. But one day my computer crashed. I still had the thumb drive, but I hadn't backed it up in weeks. Now everything is saved to the cloud."

"How protected is your cloud?"

"It's pretty secure. I mean, anything can be hacked. Do you think he plans to attack my writing?"

"I don't know, but that's a possibility. Maybe you should back everything up to a thumb drive just in case. I have an extra one floating around my computer desk. I'll get it and you can use my laptop." He pointed to the laptop sitting on the kitchen counter. After searching the computer desk, he finally found the thumb drive in the bottom drawer and returned to the kitchen where Maggie was booting up the laptop.

He sat at the table while Maggie plugged the thumb drive in.

"Everything is still here so we have averted that potential disaster. Thank you."

She saw the notebook lying next to her stack of paper towel notes. "What's that?"

"I told you I did some research last night. I jotted down some thoughts."

"May I?"

He pushed everything to her.

She chewed on her bottom lip as she read. "You know; I think there is a pattern."

"Really?" He came around the table and stood next to her. Leaning one hand on the chair behind her and the other on the table next to the note pad, he bent to get a closer look at the list. Her breath hitched at his proximity. His mind traveled to the kiss they shared last night, and he thought about an encore.

She swallowed hard and turned her attention back to the notebook in front of her. "Yes. You know, I didn't give it any thought when these things were happening, but there is a new taunt every day. I got into town on Monday, and we were shot at that night. Tuesday morning the package containing my parents' rings was delivered. Wednesday, I had lunch with Cassie and her car was vandalized. Thursday morning, I found Jacob battered on my porch. Friday was my birthday and the awful message in the hotel room. Yesterday, we found Dee's body in your car, and early this morning someone broke into the house and left the video."

"You're right. Why didn't I see that?" He straightened and walked to the sink. How had he missed that?

"The same reason I didn't. We were so focused on the what and the why that we weren't paying attention to the when."

"So, if that's the case, then we could assume that whatever he has planned won't happen until tomorrow. Since we have a whole day to anticipate his next move, do you think there would be anything at your father's house that could be used? Do you want to see if we can figure out if that move might involve your father's belongings?"

TWENTY-ONE

They had both freshened up and climbed into his truck. They were going to spend the afternoon going through her father's home office.

"I still want you to be careful. We may think our guy is doing things on a time frame, but we can't be certain. We'll go to your dad's house and go through his paperwork. See if he acquired any new property or investments."

Once they were at the house, Cody unlocked the padlock that a deputy had installed on the outside of the door after documenting the scene and collecting evidence. He closed the door behind them, moved the end table to hold it shut, and activated the alarm before doing a sweep of the house. No one was lurking in the shadows waiting to attack them.

They started in her father's office downstairs. There wasn't much to the room—an old metal desk with two drawers, a filing cabinet, an old loveseat, and a wingback chair. The far wall had a huge picture window with a small school desk below it, and the left wall displayed a built-in bookshelf.

She remembered as a young girl she'd come work at her small desk while her father worked at his. Her father would take a break and sit in the chair. He'd let her climb on his lap with one of the books from his shelf. He had titles ranging from *Moby Dick* to *The Scarlet Letter* to *The Lord of the Rings*. That room was where her love of reading had been born along with the desire to create her own stories.

She sat at her father's desk and ran her fingers over his pen collection lined up neatly. She opened the top drawer and looked through its contents. It was mostly office supplies, more pens, a stapler, staples, paper clips, and envelopes.

The second drawer contained her father's banking documents. What she hadn't known when she was younger was that the work her father was doing was really paying the bills and studying his Bible. Her eyes misted at all the memories that surfaced.

Cody had started digging through the filing cabinet. "Your father kept everything."

"Tell me about it. I found a bottle of aspirin in his bathroom that expired in 2008."

"Ouch. I sure hope he wasn't still taking those."

She laughed as she rose from the desk and crossed the room. "Have you found anything of interest?"

"Oh, yes. I've found several interesting things but nothing our guy could use. I mean, what could he do with tax returns dating back to 1988 or divorce papers from 1956?"

"Oh my goodness. He still had my grandparents' divorce papers? You've definitely beat me in the old category." She wandered to the bookshelf and picked up an anthology of Shakespeare's works. She opened it to her favorite play. She'd always giggled at Bottom's transformation.

As she had gotten older, instead of climbing in her father's lap and letting him read to her, she'd climb into the wingback chair and read quietly to herself. She was there so much her father had bought the loveseat for her so he could have his chair back.

Cody closed the bottom drawer and moved to the middle one. He looked through it while she thumbed through the books. Her dad's collection had dwindled considerably in the last few years. Most were now in her collection.

Cody closed the middle drawer and moved to the top. "Bingo."

She slid the book back onto the shelf and joined him at the cabinet.

"Here's a folder that says deeds." He pulled it out and thumbed through the pages. "There are several deeds, but they all have the same legal description. Looks like he had his own makeshift abstract on this land." He handed her the folder and went back to the drawer. "Here's a folder with your name on it and one with Jake's name."

She smiled at her father's sentimental nature. "Yep. Mine'll have old report cards, school pictures, drawings, and my writings. Jacob's file will have pretty much the same thing, except it'll also have some Army related things. Speaking of Army stuff, did you come across any of dad's?"

"Yes. I saw some discharge papers, photos, medals, and ribbons in the middle drawer."

"Good. I've got to remember where those are." She wanted to come back and spend some time looking at all those historical photos.

"What do we have here?" He pulled a picture from a file and whistled.

Could he have found something important? He turned the picture around. It was her third-grade school picture. Her hair was neatly fixed in ringlets, and she wore a bright yellow dress, which brought out the dark black circle around her eye.

"Is that sweet little Maggie sporting a shiner?" He made tsking noises.

She snatched the photo from him and stuck it back in the folder. "Yes, it is."

"Do tell." His eyebrows quirked up.

"Alexander Brown tried to kiss me on the monkey bars, so I punched him."

"If you were the one doing the punching, how did you get the black eye? Did he fight back?"

163

"No. He screamed and let go of the bars. He went down kicking. My legs got tangled up with his and took me down with him. I took an elbow to the eye on the way down."

Cody roared with laughter. "I'm glad you didn't hit me when I tried to kiss you."

"No. I was glad you did. I was starting to wonder how long it would take you." She laughed. Things grew awkward after that statement. She had been referring to the first time he kissed her. Not the most recent kiss. Was he thinking she meant that one?

Cody cleared his throat. "I'm not finding anything else."

"I didn't see anything else, either. I could us a drink. You?"

"Sure."

"Do you think there could be anything of use in the basement?" she asked Cody as they sat at the kitchen table where they had taken a break.

"It can't hurt to look. Why don't I do that, and you can search your father's room and see if there is anything there?"

Searching his office was tough, but going through his personal belongings would be harder. She had purposely stayed out of his room, other than the day when her parents' rings had been stolen, knowing the memories would be overwhelming. But if going through that stuff could lead to finding something to stop this guy, then she would do it. She'd have to pray for the strength to make it through it.

"Okay."

He stood and took the stairwell to the basement. She placed their cups in the sink, then thought better of it. She should probably wash them because there was no telling when she would get to come back.

She washed the cups and thought she needed to gather the trash so that it wouldn't start smelling while she was away. *What are you doing? There is no trash to gather, you haven't been here much. You are postponing the inevitable. Get up there and get it over with.*

Taking the stairs slowly, anxiety rose in her chest. At the top of the stairs, she saw her father's room and kept her eyes on it as she took shaky steps. She crossed the threshold and stared at the surroundings. Inhaling deeply, the room smelled of his cologne with a hint of dust. Farther into the room, she ran her hand along his dresser. It was covered with various little jars. She lifted the lid on one and it contained nothing but quarters. The next jar contained dimes and the next nickels.

Her search of the drawers didn't reveal anything other than her father's clothes. Crossing the room, she took a moment to gaze out the window. Her parents' room looked out over the garden her mother had kept for many years. Her father had kept it up after her passing. Now it was overrun with weeds. Another thing to add to the to-do list.

She turned to the closet. His favorite shirts were hanging in prominent spots. The farther back in the clothes she went the further back in time she went. She found a shirt she distinctly remembered him wearing in a photo when she was nine. She, of course, had been wearing a matching shirt. Her shirt was long gone by now.

There were boxes on an overhead shelf. She pulled them down and took them to his bed. His reading glasses laying atop his Bible on the nightstand. She touched them, hoping for one last connection. The ache in her chest was unending—a piece of her heart was missing, and she would never get it back. Tears slid down her cheeks.

She'd become a weepy mess lately.

Footsteps behind her alerted her to Cody's presence. She didn't turn around right away, instead, she wiped the tears from her eyes and busied herself looking in the boxes. She didn't want him to see her crying. Again. She cleared her throat, hoping her voice would sound normal.

"Did you find anything?"

There was no answer, just the sound of his feet shuffling into the room.

Before she could turn around and face him, a sharp pain began at the base of her neck, radiating all over her skull. Lights danced in her vision before everything faded to black.

TWENTY-TWO

After he descended the stairs into the dank basement, Cody heard Maggie moving around upstairs before she settled into complete silence. He hadn't really wanted to search the basement. He didn't think there would be anything down here, but he thought Maggie might need some time alone when she entered her father's room.

The only things down here were boxes of junk. He methodically opened the lid to every one. He found three boxes of old musty clothes, several random car parts, and lots of half-empty bottles of cleaning supplies. Two vacuum cleaners stood abandoned in the corner.

He'd gone through every box down here. Standing in the center of the basement, he turned slowly in a circle, taking in the entire basement, making sure he hadn't missed anything. Satisfied he hadn't, he looked at his watch. It had been twenty minutes. That should have given Maggie some time to come to grips with the grief he suspected she would face. It was time to go upstairs and check on her.

He climbed the old rickety basement steps and shut the door behind him. The house was eerily quiet, making the hair on his neck stand on end. There weren't any sounds coming from upstairs. His gut told him something was off, his adrenaline picked up, and he took the stairs two at a time. He called her name as he strode down the hall to Mr. Jones's room.

Maggie lay crumpled on the floor by her father's bed. Her hair was wild and covering her face. Heart racing, he feared the worse. He knelt beside her and brushed the hair from her face. He felt for a pulse, it was there, strong and steady. *Thank you, God.*

"Maggie? Can you hear me?" Why was she laying on the floor? There didn't appear to be anything out of sorts with room. Maybe she had tripped and fallen. Had she fainted?

A small moan escaped her lips.

"Come on, baby. Can you open your eyes?" He caressed her face, trying to bring her back to consciousness. "Maggie, it's me. Open your eyes." He continued to smooth his hand across her cheek.

Turning her head in the direction of his touch caused a grimace to spread across her face. Her eyes barely opened and then closed again. His pulse settled slightly as she began responding.

"It's okay, Magpie, I'm right here. Come on, open your eyes." He spoke softly. Her head turned to follow his voice.

She squinted at him.

"Are you all right?"

She stared at him for a moment, confusion marring her beautiful face. He repeated the question, and she nodded. The nod was followed by another grimace. He helped her to a standing position and led her to a chair by the window.

"Can you tell me what happened?" He brushed hair from her face so he could see her eyes.

"I don't know. I was about to go through some boxes I pulled from the closet when you came in. I asked if you'd found anything. There was a blinding pain, then I woke up to the sound of your voice."

Lifting her left hand to her head, the glint of something sparkled in the sunlight. She ran her hand through her hair, down the back of her head, and to her neck. She winced when she touched the base of her head.

"Maggie, when I came up here, you were already on the floor."

She stood abruptly, wobbling before collapsing into his arms. "I'm so dizzy."

He waited for her to steady herself against him before easing her back into the chair. "Let me look at your head." She turned in the chair, and he moved her hair. He instantly went on high alert. She'd been attacked. A deep purple bruise was already starting to form. "You took a hit to the head."

She turned back and shook her head to move her hair. Pain crossed her face, and she raised her hand back to her forehead. The sparkle caught his eye again, and his breath stopped. He grabbed her hand and pulled it closer. On her ring finger was a very familiar sapphire ring. It looked exactly like the ring he'd bought for her six years ago.

It couldn't be. His ring had to be safe at home. Maybe she had found this one among her mother's jewelry. Rings like this weren't exactly rare.

He was grasping at straws.

"Maggie, where did you get this?" He aimed her hand up so she could see the ring.

Words scribbled on the palm of her hand distracted him from her reaction. Dread filled him. Before he could confirm what it said, she yanked her hand from his and stood, walking around him unsteadily. "I don't know. I've never seen it before. How did it get on my finger?"

"Let me see your hand."

She held her hand out so he could see the ring, but it wasn't the ring he wanted to see. He turned her palm over and terror gripped him. *Eight for a Wish.*

"We need to go. Now." He pulled his gun from its holster and flipped the safety off. Using his free hand, he grabbed hers and pulled her to the doorway. He stood absolutely still, listening for any sound that might be coming from outside the room. Complete

169

silence. He slowly stuck his head around the doorframe, confirming the hallway was empty. He pulled Maggie behind him as he took off toward the stairs.

"Cody, tell me what's going on." She didn't urge him to stop. Instead, she kept pace with him as he ran down the stairs. He pushed her body against the front door and stood in front of her, forming a wall of protection around her.

"He's been here. For all we know, he's still here. We need to leave. I'm going to check out front and make sure no one's out there, then we're going to run for the truck. I want you to stay as close to me as you can."

The fear that had frequented her eyes in the last several days was back. He placed a gentle kiss on her forehead. "I'm going to get you out of here safely."

He leaned to the left and peered out the window, scanning the front yard. Nothing appeared to be out of place, and there weren't any shadows moving in the tree line. He grabbed Maggie's hand and used it to pull her behind him. He was now the wall between her and anything on the other side of that door. Pulse racing wildly, a drop of sweat rolled down his back as he opened the door and stepped out onto the porch, pulling Maggie even closer, her body melding with his. *There's no going back. One. Two. Three.*

He took off running for the truck with Maggie on his heels. There were no gunshots. No one surged from the shrubs. He opened the driver's side door and pushed Maggie in ahead of him. She scooted across the seat as he climbed in and started the truck.

"Get down, just in case." He motioned for her to crouch low. If their guy was still out there, he didn't want her in the line of fire. He slammed his foot on the accelerator and sped down the drive, leaving dirt clouds in his wake. When he turned onto the main road, Maggie sat up, looking disoriented and nauseated.

"Cody, what's going on?" She looked down at the ring on her finger. "Where did this come from?"

How did he answer that? That ring was supposed to be hidden in a drawer. His secret was about to be revealed. Why had he kept that ring? That was a question he would have to answer later. Right now, they had bigger concerns. He decided to sidestep the question.

"It was part of another attack, Magpie."

He glanced at her. She was studying the ring on her finger. She turned her palm over to take the ring off and let out a loud squeal. She'd finally found the words that had sent them running from the house.

TWENTY-THREE

There, written in red ink, were the words *Eight for a Wish*. Her fuzzy brain struggled to catch up. It hadn't been Cody in the room earlier—it had been the stalker. He must have hit her with something, put the ring on her finger, and then written those four little words.

She had to get them off. Palm down, she started viciously rubbing her hand on her pants, trying to scrub the words away. Another look proved the words remained. Licking the fingers of her right hand, she used them to wipe at her palm. She turned her hand back to her pants and scrubbed some more.

Oh, God. Please, get it off. Panic set in. Her heart raced, and her breaths came faster. Her hand was never going to be clean. The words would be there to taunt her forever. Her palm burned from the friction, but she had to rid herself of those words, even if she had to bleed to do so. Before she could begin another frantic attempt, Cody's large hand grabbed hers. She tried to pull away, but his grip was too tight.

"I have to get the words off my hand. Please, Cody." She tried to pull again, but he wouldn't release her. Her chest constricted, and her lungs fought hard for air. She took deep, labored gasps.

"Cody, please." She looked at him. His gaze was intense on the road, but he cautioned a look at the review mirror, and then back to the road. He pulled her to him so that she sat nestled at his side.

"It's okay, Maggie. Those words won't hurt you, honey."

She laid her head on his chest and listened to his heart, willing hers to match the beat. He released her hand and slowly caressed her arm. He whispered a prayer into her hair. Her breathing incrementally returned to normal. Cody's warm hand continued its comforting journey up and down her arm until her heart was no longer racing in her chest.

When she could finally speak, she sat up and moved back to her side of the truck. She immediately regretted the move. No longer feeling the warmth from Cody's body, a shiver ran up her spine.

"Thank you." Trying to move inconspicuously, she changed positions again, settling slightly closer to him.

His concentration was still on the road, but he quickly looked at her and smiled.

She removed the ring and inspected it further. It was a sapphire princess cut surrounded by smaller glittering stones, which she assumed were either cubic zirconia or possibly even diamonds. The band was simple white gold. If it weren't for the circumstances, the ring would have been beautiful.

She showed it to Cody. "Do you want to see it?"

His gaze never left the road. "Uh, I know what it looks like. I've seen it before." His words were filled with a longing she hadn't heard from him since she'd returned to Whitehaven.

"What do you mean you've seen it before? Oh, God, did it belong to Iris or Dee? Is it supposed to signify I am going to die next? Is that the wish? He wishes for my death?" She could feel another panic attack creeping up her body.

He jerked his head to face her. "No! No. It did not belong to them, and the wish isn't for your death. There's an inscription on the inside of the band. Go ahead and read it."

She brought the ring closer to her face and tilted it to read the inscription.

My Magpie. She closed her eyes and took a deep breath as the memory swamped her.

She pressed her ear to the bedroom door, listening for any sound to indicate her father had gotten up. Nothing. She quietly raced to the bedroom window, raised it, and waited again for any sounds from the hallway. After a minute of silence, she gingerly climbed out the window, tiptoed to the tree by Jacob's bedroom, and shimmied down.

The house was dark and looming in the moonlight. She'd be scared if she weren't already trembling with excitement. She jogged to the path that would lead to the pond. Cody said he'd meet her there at midnight. She turned in circles looking around. He wasn't there. The excitement started to die down and disappointment took its place. Maybe he couldn't make it.

They'd been secretly seeing each other for two weeks. Their clandestine meetings were never long enough. She wanted to be with him all the time, and it had been her idea to meet tonight. She stood next to the towering trees and waited. A snap from behind made her jump.

"Maggie?" Cody's hushed whisper calmed her fears as he emerged from the tree line.

"I was beginning to think you'd changed your mind," she teased.

"Nothing could keep me away from you." He slid his hand into hers. His touch started a blaze in her hand that spread throughout her body as he pulled her down the path. "I would have been waiting for you, but I have a surprise."

"I love surprises." She tried not to let the bubbling, girlish giggle escape. "What is it?"

"Well, if I told you, it wouldn't be a surprise." He squeezed her hand.

"I suppose not." They walked the rest of the path in silence, hand in hand.

The bright moonlight shone through the opening of the trees at the end of the path. On the other side was a clearing that contained a small pond fed by a flowing creek.

"Surprise." Cody turned her to face a large blanket spread on the ground. There were two pillows positioned a couple feet apart and a small ice chest on the edge. "The Perseid meteor shower starts tonight. I thought we could try to find a shooting star."

They walked to the blanket, and she took a seat next to one of the pillows. He sat next to her.

"What's in the ice chest?" If it had been any other boy, she'd be afraid of what was in it. Cody was different. He'd seen firsthand the damage alcohol could do.

He reached over and produced her favorite soda. "For you, my lady."

"Thank you, kind sir." She took a drink.

She laid down and rested her head on the pillow, clasping her hands over her stomach. Cody moved his pillow slightly closer to hers and laid down. He wasn't touching her, but she could feel the heat radiating from his arm inches away. She let her hand slide down to her side and searched for his. Finding it, she intertwined their fingers.

"This is nice." She stared at the sky, waiting for a star to dash across.

"It is." His voice was husky.

They laid in comfortable silence. Words weren't necessary. Being together was all they needed.

"There!" He let go of her hand and pointed as a light darted across the sky.

"I see it!" The thrill of catching a glimpse of a shooting star danced in her heart.

"Now we have to make a wish. Close your eyes."

She closed her eyes. What could she wish for? She had everything she wanted. At least, things she could have. Wishing on a star wasn't going to bring her mother back. She'd wish for more moments like this. She was free and content, and she was certain the boy next to her could be thanked for that.

She opened her eyes to find he had rolled on to his side, his head propped on his hand, watching her.

"My Magpie." His voice was as soft as the look on his face. He leaned down and tenderly kissed her. His soft lips sent chills through her while setting her on fire at the same time. Her stomach quaked as he deepened the kiss.

The ring slipped from her hand and fell to her lap, snapping her from her memories. This ring had been meant for her. She was completely certain. Not today, and not from a stalker, but six years ago from Cody. She was speechless. She didn't know what to think much less what to say.

"Cody. What does this mean?"

The muscles along his strong jaw twitched. He didn't say anything, didn't even look at her. He kept staring straight ahead, watching the road. What about this ring made him go silent? Why did he have it? Even if he had planned on giving it to her years ago, why hadn't he gotten rid of it after he sent her away? Maybe he had been completely honest when he said he broke up with her because he thought that was what was best for her. He hadn't been playing with her heart back then.

"It means that this isn't about just you."

"I'm not sure I understand. I was the one knocked out, this ring placed on my finger, and those awful words written on my hand. Who else is it about?"

"That ring you have in your hands was locked safely away in my bedroom."

"Why do you have this ring? This is… from before, right?" She needed to know the story behind the ring and behind the inscription. His terse nod was barely visible. "Why do you still have it?"

His jaw tensed and started moving back and forth. He was grinding his teeth. His Adam's apple bobbed.

"Cody."

She wanted to hear him say it. His grip tightened on the steering wheel, and he let out a sigh. "That night, the one when I told you good-bye… I'd had that in my pocket all day. I was going to give it to you after we told Jake and your dad about us. It was going to be my promise to you. My promise to love you until we were old and gray."

Everything clicked into place. "That was your wish that night we saw the falling star."

He nodded. "I had *My Magpie* engraved on it."

"Why? You knew how much I hated that name."

"I know. To you, Magpie was a silly nickname we gave you about an annoying, loud, little bird. But that wasn't the meaning to me. I, uh, had to do a particularly boring history project before I graduated. Did you know the people of the Manchu Dynasty believed that the Magpie brought good luck? Well, that's what you were to me. You were my good luck."

She looked down at the ring and ran a finger around the circle of clear stones that haloed the sapphires. *I would have said yes.* "*Eight for a wish* is for both of us. I don't understand."

"Someone has been in my house. They know enough about our past to understand what that ring means, what you mean to me. The attack today also means that he's not sticking to a schedule, so we can't know when he'll strike next."

"Where are we going to go now? This person obviously knows enough about us to know of any places that we could hide. They somehow know small, intimate details about both of us. How could they know that? Cody, did you tell anyone about the ring?"

He shook his head. "There were a few people around town that knew we were dating. The jewelry store where I bought the ring and the florist where I had bought your birthday flowers. In a particularly nasty fight with my mother, I let it slip that I was seeing you, but she had been drunk as usual and didn't remember the fight the next morning. We need to disappear." He drummed his fingers on the steering wheel. "Do you have your cell phone?"

She started at his sudden question. She fished her phone from her pocket and tried to hand it to him, but he shook his head.

"I think whoever is behind this might be using our phones to track our whereabouts. I want you to call your brother, briefly tell him what's going on. Tell him I'm taking you somewhere safe and we'll be in touch. And then turn your phone off and take the battery out."

She followed his instructions without argument. She dialed Jacob as Cody pulled his cell phone from his pocket. He called Grainger while she called Jacob. When she ended the call, she removed the battery from her phone. Cody had her do the same with his.

"There's a campground that straddles the county line. It's not just a campground. They offer cabins for rent. I think that may be the best place to go. We have to assume that any place that has a connection to either one of us has the potential to be dangerous."

"Just take me somewhere safe." Pain pounded in her temples. She wanted this nightmare to be over. He slowed and pulled into the parking lot of a truck stop, right before the Dale County border.

"How's your head?" he asked, turning to face her.

"It hurts, but I'll make it."

"Why don't we go in and get some medicine for the pain?"

She nodded and got out of the truck. He followed her into the truck stop.

"I need to use the bathroom." She followed the sign pointing the way to the restrooms, Cody right on her heels. "You don't have to go with me."

"I'm not letting you out of my sight. I've done that once today and look what happened."

She stopped, spinning around and pinning him with her wide eyes. "Excuse me?"

"Well, not for long any way." His cheeks were red with embarrassment. He grinned as he grabbed her shoulders, spinning her back around and giving her a small shove toward the restrooms.

He was leaning against the wall by the restroom door when she exited five minutes later.

"It took some scrubbing, but I finally got those words off my hand." She was absentmindedly rubbing at the palm of her hand even though it was clean.

They walked down the sundry aisle and picked up a bottle of pain reliever.

"I need to get a drink; I can't take pills without it."

"We should probably get a few drinks and snacks to hold us over until we can do proper shopping for the cabin."

She pulled her debit card from her purse and started to hand it to the cashier. It was a good thing she had left her purse in the truck when they had stopped at her father's house.

"No debit cards. We don't want to leave an electronic trail. I've got some cash." He pulled his wallet from his pocket and paid cash for their items. They walked out of the truck stop.

There was something flapping in the wind under the windshield wiper. She hated when people distributed fliers like that, but she hated it even more when people threw them on the ground. He pulled the flier from the windshield and turned it over.

TWENTY-FOUR

He looked down at the paper. It was a black and white photo of two people in the middle of a passionate kiss. Closer inspection revealed that it wasn't two random people. It was them. A photo of the kiss they had shared in her father's house that morning. Written across the image in large red letters were the words *Nine for a Kiss*.

"Get in the truck. Now." His tone left no room for argument. Neither did the speed in which he got into the truck and fired up the engine.

She was in the truck and barely had the door closed before he was flying out of the parking spot. "What's going on?" Fear colored her words.

He reached onto the dash, grabbed the flier he had thrown up there when he climbed into the truck, and thrust it at her. "This isn't a flier."

Her hand went to her mouth. "Who took this?"

"I don't know. I searched the entire house and didn't find anyone before I came to your room this morning."

If there wasn't anyone in the house, how had someone taken a picture of their kiss? Had he missed something in his search?

"Do you think they installed cameras in the house?"

"That would explain how he knew we were at the house today, in separate rooms even. But it doesn't explain how he got in or how he knew we were at the truck stop. I am positive we weren't followed, and we turned off our cell phones so it couldn't be those. My only other idea is that there is a tracking device on the truck."

He slammed his palm on the steering wheel. Someone was going through a lot of trouble to follow her. They'd probably placed cameras in her father's house and now a possible tracking device on the rental truck. *There's probably a tracking device on her father's truck, too, and maybe even Jake's vehicle.*

"Do you have a plan? I mean, if there's a tracking device on the truck, this guy will be able to follow us where ever we go."

He was silent for a moment, his gaze glued to the road ahead. He looked in the rearview mirror and stared for a moment. A small white truck was not too far behind them. He'd seen the truck idling at a gas pump when they drove off.

He signaled to turn right on to the next road. He made the turn effortlessly, and once he had the truck straightened, he glanced in the mirror again. The truck was still on their tail. A few blocks up, he made another right turn, this time without signaling. Another glance in the rear-view mirror showed the white truck did the same.

Maggie turned around to see what was going on. "Do you think they're following us?"

"I'm not sure, but we're about to find out." Without slowing down or using his turn signal, Cody abruptly turned right. The white truck made the same turn and gunned it. Whoever it was, he or she knew they were on to them.

Cody revved the engine and pushed the speedometer higher. He let off the accelerator and did another impromptu right hand turn back out onto the highway. He held his breath as the truck started gaining on them. "Hold on." They were already doing well above the speed limit.

She grabbed the door handle as the white truck pushed into the bed of their truck, slamming her against the seatbelt. She screamed at the sound of crunching metal.

The truck pulled into the lane next to them and started to pass them. Crossing into their lane, it made contact with the passenger's side. His arms burned with the exertion of trying to keep them from being pushed into the ditch.

He turned the wheel to the right and fought to stay on the road. He slammed on the brakes, slowing their truck. The assaulting truck kept going, crossed in front of them, and ended up driving onto the shoulder. Cody made a U-turn and sped off in the direction they had come from.

"Are you okay?" He glanced at her before turning his attention back to the road. His goal now was to lose their pursuer and make it safely to the sheriff's station. He loosened his grip on the steering wheel. His fingers ached as the muscles relaxed.

"I'm scared, but I'm not hurt."

He glanced in the rearview mirror, and his shoulders tensed. "Okay, this isn't over. The truck has turned around and is catching back up to us. I need you to put the battery back in my cell phone and call Grainger. At this point, we're not worried about being followed seeing as he is trying to drive us off the road." Maggie opened the glove box and started messing with the phone.

Their attacker was on top of them again. Cody pressed the pedal to the floor, praying no one would pull out from a side street not knowing what was going on. The truck made contact again, jarring them violently, causing Maggie to drop the phone on to the floor. She bent over to pick it up when they were hit again, sending her head slamming into the dashboard. She sat up and looked out the rear window and back to him. Her ashen face only multiplied his fear.

The truck started to pass them, but instead of coming flush with them and trying to push them off the road like before, it merged into their lane aiming for the rear end. He was attempting a maneuver used by police to end chases. The only way to avoid it was to increase their speed before contact was made. He pressed the accelerator all the way to the floor, and they lurched forward before their pursuer could make contact.

The white truck swerved behind them, narrowly missing leaving the roadway. Maggie bent over again to try and retrieve the phone from the floorboard.

He didn't recognize the truck, and he couldn't see the driver's face, but one thing was clear—whoever they were dealing with had had defensive driving training. Luckily for Cody, he'd also had defensive driving classes and was able to avoid it.

He mashed the accelerator, watching the needle creep higher and higher, pushing the truck as fast as it would go. He looked at Maggie; she was bent over, trying desperately to reach the phone that had fallen. If anything happened to her, he wouldn't be able to forgive himself.

In the split second it took for him to check on her, their pursuer was able to correct his trajectory and was closing back in on them. Their pursuer got in position to attempt another PIT maneuver. As the truck inched closer, Cody deliberately increased his speed, but the pursuer predicted that and sped up as well. The driver's side quarter panel made contact with the passenger's side of the truck bed, and it started to spin. He let off the accelerator and turned the wheels into the spin to avoid flipping over. The front end of the white truck smashed into Maggie's side. The sounds of breaking of glass and Maggie's shrill scream chilled his veins. This was the end.

The impact hurled them off the road and into a wooden fence that was along the road. His head crashed into the driver's side window, shattering it right before he lost consciousness.

* * * *

He opened his eyes. Everything was blurry. How long had he been unconscious? Blinking several times, he was able to determine it

184

wasn't his vision but a fine dust filling the cabin. The only thing he could hear was the running motor.

"Maggie?" He whispered her name as he tried to stop his head from spinning. She didn't answer. Turning toward her, he could see she was still safely belted into the passenger's seat. The airbags had deployed and were laying limply in her lap. Outside the window, the white truck that had pushed them off the road was nowhere to be seen. Had it driven off?

Cody unbuckled and tried to open his door, but it wouldn't budge. *Of course, it's not going to open, you're shoved up against a fence.*

"Maggie?" He leaned over and clumsily felt for a pulse on her wrist. *Please God, let her be okay.* A steady thump beat under his fingers. She was still alive, but there was no telling what kind of injuries she had sustained. He needed to get her to a hospital.

"Hey, man! Are you guys all right?" The voice was familiar, but Cody wasn't sure where he'd heard it before. He leaned his head against the headrest, battling the pain and confusion, trying to gather his thoughts.

"Cody, is that you?" the voice called from the driver's side. Cody turned in time to see a hand come in the window and then there was a sharp pinch on his neck.

"Hey!" His hand went to where he felt the pinch, but there was nothing there. He started feeling woozy. The world spun around him, and his eyes drifted closed, but he forced them open. He squinted, trying to bring the face into focus, but he couldn't get a clear picture.

"Ten for something you won't want to miss."

"Magpie," Cody said weakly as he turned to protect her. Darkness consumed him before he could reach her.

TWENTY-FIVE

Cody's voice pulled at her from somewhere in the fog she was currently residing in. She opened her eyes and allowed them to adjust to the lighted room. Cody sat on a bed across from her. What had happened? All she could remember was the truck turning and her head hitting the glass. Everything else was blank.

Something heavy weighed her arm down. A three-inch silver band circled her wrist, a long thick metal chain attached to the band. She slowly followed it to where it was fastened to the wall with large screws.

She was secured to a wall, but she didn't panic. All she could concentrate on was the pain. She couldn't ever remember being in this much pain. Her head was going to explode, and the muscles in her neck and back screamed with each movement. She forced herself to focus on Cody's face and not on the pain. His hair was mussed, and he had something smeared on his forehead. He didn't look as bad as she felt.

"Maggie, are you okay?"

She opened her mouth to speak, but the words wouldn't come, her mouth was like cotton. She swallowed several times before she was able to respond. "I think so. What about you?"

"I've felt better."

"What happened? Where are we?"

"We wrecked. You were unconscious and then…" He paused, like he was trying to decide how to tell her some bad news.

Before he could finish his sentence, they heard a key in the lock on the door to her right. It opened slowly inward. Her view of who had entered was obscured by the door.

"How could you?" Cody's rage-filled voice yelled. "I trusted you!" Metal clanged as he stood and lunged at their captor, but he didn't get very far before his own chain snapped him back to the bed.

"I could say the same thing to you, Sheriff." The voice was filled with disdain. She knew that voice. She had heard it several times in the last week, but she couldn't pinpoint who it belonged to. The door opened wider, revealing a man dressed in a Dale County Sheriff's uniform. He turned to face her. "Hello, Magpie."

She cringed as Deputy Grainger called her the name only Cody and Jacob used. "Why?" was all she could say. She had never met Grainger before this week. She had no idea why he would target her so maliciously.

"There'll be plenty of time for questions later." He walked over and stopped in front of her. She fought the urge to cower away from his looming figure. He tucked a strand of her auburn hair behind her ear. It was a comforting gesture when Cody did it, but her stomach revolted at Grainger's touch.

She slapped his hand away. Her gesture of defiance was rewarded with a slap across her cheek. His hand was hard and left her cheek stinging. The assault stunned her. No one had ever hit her like that. She fought back the tears that threatened to spill. Cody was yelling at him, standing, and trying to pull the chain from the wall to get to her.

Deputy Grainger wasn't fazed by Cody's reaction. He reached behind him and produced a pair of handcuffs. Grabbing the hand that wasn't chained to the wall, he slapped a cuff on her, tightening it until it pinched her skin. He reached for her other hand, but she refused to let him have it, scooting back on the bed until she felt the wall behind her. He leaned over to grab the chain attached to the wall, and she tried to kick him away. He blocked her kick with his hand and raised his other hand to slap her again but paused before making contact. Instead, he took his service weapon from its holster and aimed it at Cody.

"No!" The air was sucked from her lungs and pounding sounded in her ears. She straightened her body, forcing her shaky limbs to cooperate. "I'll do what you want."

"Maggie, no," Cody yelled from his side of the room. "Don't do it."

Deputy Grainger kept the gun aimed at Cody but turned to her. "You can fight me, and I'll put a bullet in your boyfriend, then make you come with me anyway. Or you can come with me willingly, and I let him live."

"Please, don't hurt him," she pleaded.

"Then put the other cuff on your hand."

She did as she was told. Once the cuff was secured on her wrist, Grainger tightened it. "Wouldn't want you to escape."

He holstered his weapon and pulled a key from his pocket. Unlocking the small lock attached to the cuff, he freed her from the wall before grabbing her upper arm and pulling her to a standing position. She gasped in pain. He dragged her toward the door. "Walk."

"Grainger, she hasn't done anything to you. Take me instead."

Maggie could hear the desperation in Cody's voice. She saw the fear in his eyes as she walked toward the door.

"Sorry, I can't do that." He shoved her through the door, shutting it behind him, never releasing her arm.

"*Grainger!*" Cody's guttural yell echoed as Grainger relocked the door.

He pulled her down a dark hallway that opened to a larger room with cement walls. There was a washer and dryer in the corner and a set of stairs that led up to a closed door. There were windows situated at the top of the walls, similar to the previous room she was in, only they were dingy and didn't let much light through. A single lightbulb in the center of the large room gave her enough light to recognize that she was in the basement of a building.

He remained silent as he pushed her to the stairs. Her fear grew with each step. She didn't know where he was taking her or what he was going to do. Hesitating, she said a silent prayer. *Lord, be with me. I don't know what the future holds but You do, Lord. I'm so scared, but I know that You are with me.*

"Go up." His gravelly voice wasn't as harsh as it had been moments ago, but it wasn't as friendly as it had been in every exchange prior to today. With shaky steps, she climbed.

She didn't know where Grainger was taking her or what he planned to do to her, but she wasn't going to give up without a fight. She walked up and through the door, which opened into a small kitchen furnished with a stove and refrigerator. Pots and pans hung on the wall over the stove and various kitchen appliances lined the countertops. *This isn't a vacant home; someone is living here. Maybe there's a phone I can use to call for help if I can break away from Grainger.* She looked around the kitchen and couldn't find a phone but did see a knife block to her left. When Grainger's attention was on shutting the basement door, Maggie used the distraction as her chance for escape. She pulled a knife from the block and turned to face Grainger. He stared at her, and then he laughed.

"You're not serious?" He pulled the gun from its holster and waved it at her. "I have a gun and you," using the gun to gesture to the weapon she held in her hand, "have a vegetable peeler."

She looked in her hand and sure enough, she had picked a small paring knife.

"First, you would have to get really close to do any harm with that, and second, you come at me and I'll put a bullet in you. Now, put it down. I really don't want to get any blood on the kitchen floor."

She didn't want to let go of her only protection. She knew he was right, but setting it down was like giving in to death.

Grainger aimed the gun at her leg. "One."

She quickly ran through her options and no matter what she came up with, it didn't end well for her. She set the knife on the counter.

"Good girl." Keeping the gun aimed on her, he moved the knife out of reach, and then he struck her again. "Do *not* do that again. I won't be so nice next time. Now, turn around and walk through that door." He jammed the gun in her back as he pushed her toward the other room.

Her cheek stung where his hand had connected to the already sore flesh. She brought her cuffed hands to her cheek, choking back tears.

The kitchen connected to a modest living room. He shoved her down onto a couch positioned against the wall. Her gaze traveled the room, taking in her surroundings. A coffee table was situated between the couch and a television along the opposite wall, positioned in front of a large picture window. To the left of the window was a door leading out of the house.

Grainger sat next to her on the couch, so close she could smell the stale cologne he wore. He picked up a photo album off the coffee table and opened it, placing it on her lap.

She stared down at pictures of a girl and boy playing on the beach. The boy was about eight and the girl a year or two younger. In one picture, they were splashing around in the ocean. The next picture showed the children building a sandcastle. The following one was the little girl shoveling sand over the boy as he laid in a hole they had probably dug to bury each other.

"That was our family vacation to Florida when I was eight. Iris was almost seven." He turned more pages showcasing their family vacation. Pages upon pages of photos of the two children laughing and having fun. Then some with one or both of their parents joining in on the merriment.

He turned the pages slowly, giving her plenty of time to see each photo. She looked away, not wanting to see anymore. She looked around, trying to get a better lay out of the room and her best chance of escape.

Grainger slammed his fist down on the album, causing her to jump and sending it to the floor. "Look at what you've done." He screamed while picking it up from the floor. He placed it back on her lap. He grabbed her face and forced her to look at the photos. "Look at them!" His face was crimson, and his eyes were wild with rage.

She looked back down. When he turned the last page, he closed the album and opened another, placing that on her lap, too. This one contained pictures of the same children dressed as Mary and Joseph, probably three years later. Their faces beamed with the joy of Christmas. He flipped through this one, not saying a word. She fought hard to keep her attention on the photos. Grainger seemed to be teetering on the edge, and she didn't want to do anything to push him over.

With each turn of the page, the children continued to grow. The next album showed a handsome young Grainger in a cap and gown posing with a beautiful young woman, who Maggie assumed was Iris. The next page was Iris's graduation and various photos of her smiling and happy.

"Why are you showing me these?"

"To show you why you have to die."

Maggie's stomach turned. She was going to die, and she didn't even know why. "Why? I haven't done anything to you."

"You have to die to show our incompetent sheriff what it's like to lose someone he loves knowing he could have prevented it."

Grainger picked up a remote that was lying on the coffee table and turned on the television. A video of the inside of a house started playing. The shaky video led down a hallway and through a doorway into a room that was decorated in soft purples. The camera focused on a body lying in the center of a bed. The camera moved closer and focused on a woman she recognized from the photos. The camera zoomed in on her face. Her eyes were opened wide, but they were dull and lifeless like Dee's had been. The camera slowly panned over her entire body. Except for a burn scar on her collar bone, there were no bruises or marks to indicate a struggle. The camera traveled the length of her arm and came to rest on several pill bottles strewn about the bedspread.

"It's not Cody's fault Iris killed herself." She turned to focus on Grainger.

"It is his fault, and he's going to pay for it."

The video travelled back to Iris's face. Grainger paused the video and grabbed her face, forcing her to look at the screen. His grip was tight, fingers digging into the flesh of her cheeks. "Look at her. See how beautiful she was."

"Cody couldn't do his job, and she killed herself because of it. My baby sister is dead because of your stupid, useless boyfriend." He let go of her face.

"I'm sorry that he's forced me to do those awful things to you. I'm sorry he's forcing me to kill you."

He slammed the remote down on the coffee table. "Had he just found the guy stalking her, this wouldn't be happening. It took me a few months, but I found the guy who did it, and I took care of that problem. Cody had the entire sheriff's department at his disposal and still couldn't do it. Now he's going to have four deaths on his conscience."

Maggie, fearing that he would kill her soon, jumped from the couch and ran to the door. Using her cuffed hands, she yanked on the knob, but it wouldn't open. She fumbled with the deadbolt, but just as it unlocked, something hard hit the back of her head, sending lights dancing in her vision. And then the darkness clouded in.

TWENTY-SIX

Cody had lunged from the bed, trying to chase after Grainger, but the chain pulled him back onto the bed. The door shut, and the click of the lock was so final. He let out a groan of rage and despair.

This was it. He was never going to see Maggie again, and it was all his fault. He hadn't protected her like he had promised. And now another woman was going to die because of him. Not just any woman, but the woman he loved.

His head fell back against the wall with a thud. How could he have missed it? Grainger had been behind everything this whole time. Now that he knew, little things came trickling back to him. Grainger had been the first to arrive at Maggie's house the night they were shot at. It was because he was the shooter. That explained why Luna had gotten confused.

He'd done a walkthrough of Maggie's house, giving him the perfect opportunity to place some cameras. He'd probably used the cameras to figure out the alarm codes. The blown tire had been a ruse to get to Maggie's hotel room and leave the message on her bed.

He let out a frustrated scream. Maggie's words from their breakfast echoed in his head. She was right. He wasn't to blame for Iris's suicide, and he wasn't to blame for Grainger's actions. *I can't sit here and mope. Maggie's death at the hands of Grainger is not inevitable. I can still do something about it.*

With renewed determination, he turned and grasped the chain with both hands and positioned himself to have the best leverage. *One. Two. Three.* He pulled with everything in him, without success. He let the chain slack a tad before yanking and pulling again, using his entire body. Every muscle screamed with tension, but it didn't do any good. He pulled until his arms were weak with exertion. He grunted through gritted teeth with every pull. Sweat rolled down his forehead.

Lord, please keep Maggie safe. Be with me and help me find a way to get to her. Sitting back down on the bed, he inspected the cuff around his wrist. It was an old metal one, three inches in width. The connecting chain was soldered on. Maybe he could break the cuff from the chain. He ran his hand between the mattress and the wall, searching for something, anything, he could use to free himself. The bed was made of what appeared to be durable metal. He felt under the mattress and confirmed that there was a metal edge slightly raised, just enough to keep the mattress from sliding off the frame.

He knelt in front of the bed and raised the mattress enough to access the edge. He grasped the lock as tight as he could and positioned the metal joint on the raised edge. He raised it up and then slammed the soldered portion down as hard as he could. Nothing. He tried a couple more times, each time with more force, and each time unsuccessful.

Breaking the cuff from the chain was not going to work. Maybe removing the chain from the wall would be more successful. He inspected the metal plate that attached the chain to the wall. Using his thumb and forefinger, he tried every screw, hoping he would be able to loosen them by hand, but it was no use. He laid on his back and delivered several well-placed kicks to the chain. All his efforts were rewarded with failure.

His whole body ached from everything that had happened in the last few hours. The wreck, the drug Grainger had injected into him, and his brutal attempts to free himself. Thoughts of what

Grainger could be doing propelled him from the bed. He wasn't going to give up. He was going to find a way to free himself and then find Maggie.

He knelt back down in front of the bed and inspected the bed frame. It was the kind found in Army barracks. Maybe it was damaged somewhere, and he could pry a piece of metal free and use it as a weapon, if not to free himself. The frame was intact, though. No broken pieces, no sharp edges, nothing to aid in his escape. He lifted the mattress and found exactly what he had been searching for.

Underneath, there was a grid of wire attached to the bed with springs. If Cody could get a one loose, maybe he could straighten the edge and use it to pick the lock on the cuffs. He leaned the mattress against the wall and worked on freeing a spring.

The key in the lock alerted him to Grainger's return. He swiftly threw the mattress back down before sitting on the bed. Grainger swung the door open and stood in the threshold with Maggie thrown over his shoulder. Cody's heart plummeted. She wasn't moving. He sprang from the bed, intending to disable Grainger and get to Maggie, but the cuff digging into his arm as he stretched toward them wouldn't let him go any farther.

Grainger smirked, walked into the room, and threw Maggie's motionless body on the bed she'd occupied earlier. He turned and looked Cody square in the eye. "This is your fault. You're to blame, remember that." He left the room again, locking them in silence.

"Oh, Maggie, my Magpie." Tears pricked the corners of his eyes, and his chest was heavy with grief. Overcome with panic, he pulled at the chains over and over, using all his strength. The cuffs dug into his flesh. She still wasn't moving. He needed to get to her.

Calm down. You're no good to her when you're upset and erratic. He took several long, deep breaths. He focused on Maggie. Her chest heaved up and then slowly back down. She was breathing. He watched her chest a bit longer. Inhale, exhale. Inhale, exhale.

Thank you, God!

She was okay for now. He didn't know what Grainger had done to her or if she would be okay for much longer, and his freedom was even more important now. He lifted the mattress again and grabbed a wire, giving it a tug, and it moved some. He grasped the closest grid wire and pulled it to the spring. There was just enough give that he could possibly unhook the spring from the frame.

He worked quickly to remove the springs exposing the wires. Taking a wire, he bent it until it was pointing straight up, and then he positioned the lock above the wire, guiding it into the lock of his cuff. He moved it around, hoping to move the pins enough to unlock himself. Minutes passed and nothing. He tried again with the same result.

He leaned back against the bed frame and looked heavenward. *Lord, You know I love her. Please don't let me fail her again.* His fingers were raw, but despite the pain, he turned back around and attempted to unlock the lock. He inserted the wire and jiggled, and as he was about to give up, he heard the satisfying click of the lock unlocking.

He shook the cuff from his hand and raced to Maggie's side. He could still see the rise and fall of her chest. Her face was pale except for a purple bruise that was beginning to form on her cheek where Grainger had struck her. He had been utterly helpless in protecting her then, but he was not going to let it happen again.

Her skin was soft and warm under his hand as he cupped her uninjured cheek. "Maggie, can you hear me? It's Cody, I'm here with you."

She didn't respond, and there was no movement. No change in breathing patterns, just silence. He ran his hand down her arm and to her hands still cuffed in front of her. He grabbed one of her hands and squeezed it as he leaned over and whispered in her ear, "Hang on for me, Maggie. I love you."

A tear slid down his cheek. He couldn't lose her now. "Come on, Maggie." Bending over, he softly kissed her cheek and then laid his head against hers. He breathed in deeply, inhaling her sweet scent. "Please, God." That's all he could say. He didn't have the words to pray. God knew his heart, knew that it was broken and crying out in its own painful prayer.

TWENTY-SEVEN

Something warm caressed Maggie's cheek, and a familiar deep voice called to her, willing her to come back to him. "Magpie. I love you. Please wake up," The voice, full of agony, pleaded.

She opened her eyes and stared into stunning blue eyes hovering above her.

"Oh, Maggie, thank God."

How had she gotten back to Cody? The last thing she remembered was trying to escape from the front door.

Helping her sit up, Cody positioned himself on the bed and wrapped his arm around her, pulling her into his broad chest. "Did he hurt you?"

"I tried to get a knife while I was in the kitchen, and he struck me again. He told me he was sorry. He said I was going to die to teach you a lesson." His change in demeanor, the apology, and the remorse she could see in his eyes had confused her. Moments before she was afraid for her life, but sitting there with him in that living room, she'd almost felt sorry for him. He truly believed that Cody was forcing him to do these horrible things, that Cody deserved punishment and the only way to accomplish that was to kill her.

"Sorry is just a word. It doesn't mean anything since he brought you back down here unconscious. We've got to get out of here before he comes back."

"I tried to get a good look around while he had me upstairs."

"Upstairs?"

"Yes. We're in a basement. Right outside the door is a hallway that leads to the main basement area. There are stairs that lead up into a small kitchen. Through the kitchen is the living room, and the front door is on the far side of the living room. There were curtains on all the windows, so I couldn't see outside. The basement has windows like that one." She gestured to the rectangular window at the top of the wall. "But unlike this one, the others didn't let in light. They must have been covered by bushes or something."

"That's how we're going to get out of here. It's wide enough that we should be able to slip out. Can you walk?"

Her neck and head still screamed with excruciating pain, and she felt a little disoriented from what must be the result of head trauma, but nothing was going to stop her from walking out of there. She didn't want to leave the comfort of Cody's arms, but she knew they couldn't stay there. Standing, she took a tentative step away from the bed. Cody was by her side, waiting to catch her if she fell. Her steps, slow at first, were steady. Her legs weren't weak, and her body wasn't sluggish.

"That's good. Once we get out, we're going to have to move fast." He walked over to the rectangular window. "This window is big enough for us to crawl through. The best I can tell, the window is decorative and has no way to actually open. We'll have to break the glass."

He raised his arm to show her, and she was stunned at the sight of his wrist. She crossed the room and pulled his arm down with her still cuffed hands to get a better look. An ugly bruise wrapped itself around his wrist with cuts at the top and bottom edge of the discolored band.

"When he took you, I was afraid I'd never see you again. When he brought you back, he dumped your body on the bed, said it was my fault, and left."

"He wants you to suffer."

He waited for her to explain.

"While he had me upstairs, he pulled out some old family photo albums. He showed me pictures of Iris through the years. He talked about how he had to watch her suffer while she was being stalked. He blames you for her suicide."

His eyes clouded over with sadness. She wasn't completely sure why Deputy Grainger believed Iris's suicide was Cody's fault, but he did.

"We need to get out of here. We can talk about all of that later. Are you ready?"

Was she ready? She wanted to get as far away from here as possible, but she was terrified of what was beyond the window. Staring at the window, she started thinking of all the things that could go wrong. Shaking her head, she emptied her mind of those thoughts and focused on one minute at a time. "As ready as I'll ever be."

"Since your hands are still cuffed, I'm going to break the window and give you a boost. The sound will draw Grainger, so we have to move fast. When you're out, I want you to run. Don't look back, run as far and as fast as you can. I'll be right behind you."

He ripped strips of fabric from the mattress and wrapped them around his fist. Stepping up to the window, he punched it with his wrapped hand, sending shards of glass all over the place. Using his still covered hand, he ran it around the edges of the window, ridding the edge of jagged remnants.

Once the glass was cleared from the frame, he crouched a bit and intertwined his hands, creating a foothold to give her a boost. Maggie put her foot in his hands, and he thrust her up. She started her climb through the window, using her upper body to pull. When she was free, she stood, dusted the glass shards from her arms the best she could, and turned to help Cody.

A gunshot split the air.

"Run!" Cody yelled before he collapsed out of sight.

TWENTY-EIGHT

Searing pain tore through Cody's thigh, crumpling him to the floor. He rolled around, waiting on the next shot and the inevitable pain. Instead, Grainger stood in the doorway, gun aimed at his chest.

If Grainger shot him now, Maggie wouldn't have a chance. He had to do everything in his power to stay alive and give her time to get away. He stood, gritting his teeth through the pain and lunged at Grainger. He slammed his shoulder into Grainger's abdomen, sending them both barreling to the floor with a thud. Cody landed on top and scrambled to straddle him, delivering a swift punch to his jaw.

He glanced at the window to make sure Maggie had run and wasn't standing there watching their scuffle. He had a millisecond of relief before blinding pain emerged from the back of his head. The gun. Grainger had used it to pistol whip him. Cody's adrenaline spiked as he turned back to Grainger. He grabbed Grainger's wrist and shoved it to the side. Not a moment too soon, either. A deafening blast erupted, causing his ears to ring. Grainger bucked and rolled Cody on to his back so that Grainger was now on top. He delivered a brutal blow. Pain shot up Cody's face and connected to the pain pounding the back of his head.

Grainger *couldn't* win. Maggie hadn't had enough time to get a good head start.

Wasting no time, Grainger stood and aimed the gun at his head. "Give it up. I know what you're doing." Kneeling, he placed the barrel of the gun against the wound in Cody's leg and applied pressure.

Stars dancing in his eyes, Cody held back the howl of pain waiting to escape. He wasn't going to give Grainger the satisfaction.

"You're trying to waste time to give your little girlfriend a head start." He lifted the gun and placed the barrel against Cody's other leg. "Get up or I'll give you a matching wound."

Cody knew that having a bullet wound in one leg disadvantaged him, a second wound would render him useless. He did as he was told, standing and putting his weight on his good leg.

Using his gun, Grainger gestured to the room they had just left. "Get back in there."

Cody had to think of something. He couldn't be locked in that room and allow Grainger to go after Maggie. His gaze darted around the room, looking for something he could use to his advantage.

"Don't get any bright ideas, Sheriff. Maggie is safe. For now." He snickered as he gave Cody a shove through the door. "We're out in the middle of nowhere. I have plenty of time to deal with you and then hunt her down before she can find help."

Cody turned to face the man that had been terrorizing Maggie. He was baffled at how such a good deputy could have turned so evil.

Grainger pushed him down onto the bed and leaned against the door frame, keeping the gun aimed at him. "It's your fault. I did all of this because of you. It's your fault Iris is dead."

"How is it my fault? She killed herself. I did not give her those pills."

"It is your fault!" Spittle spewed from Grainger's mouth as he stood straighter, eyes ablaze.

"You didn't find the guy who was terrorizing her. Did you know that she was scared to open her front door every morning? Afraid of whatever note or present he would leave for her. And then after the attack, she wouldn't leave the house. I'd hear her cry every morning in the bathroom as she looked in the mirror and saw the branding that she was left with. I sat and watched her suffer silently."

The fire in his eyes morphed to agony. "She was a shell of the woman I knew and loved. And it was all because you were incompetent at your job."

Cody remembered every interview he had done with Iris after she would receive the "gifts" left by some stranger. With each report, she grew less anxious and panicked. "I did everything I could, and you know that."

"No! No, you didn't." He punched Cody's face again. Pain sliced through his lip, and a metallic taste filled his mouth. He fought back the urge to rush him again. As long as Grainger had the gun, he had the upper hand.

"You were there for everything. You know I did."

"You should have caught the guy. If you had done your job, she would still be here. The day she died, I promised myself I'd let you see how it felt to watch someone you love suffer. I knew Maggie would be back in town to wrap up her father's house. Her father's death was perfect timing."

Guilt gnawed at Cody. Iris's case still bothered him. He had done everything to catch her stalker, but they couldn't get a lead on the guy. "I'm sorry, Grainger. I really am, but why?"

"How did it feel watching her suffer?" A sadistic grin filled Grainger's face. "Seeing fear make itself at home in her eyes. Knowing there was nothing you could do to make it go away. No words that would ease her anxiety."

"If you knew this, knew the feeling and knew what Iris felt, why would you inflict that on someone else?"

"To punish everyone responsible for her death." Grainger waived the gun wildly.

"Dee? Was she responsible?"

"She was easy to manipulate." He shrugged. "I only had to pay a little extra attention to her. Tell her what a fool you were to let her go and how lucky I was that you let her go."

"*You* were her new boyfriend? You toyed with her heart and emotions to punish me, and then you killed her in cold blood." Fury boiled to the surface. Cody needed to control his emotions. The wrong move now could be catastrophic for him and Maggie.

Sadness crossed over Grainger's features. "No, she started having second thoughts. I couldn't let her mess it up. Her death was perfect for six, don't you think?" And just like that, the sadness was gone.

"What about the person that was really responsible? Doesn't he deserve this more than me or Maggie?" Not that Cody wanted Grainger to take the law into his own hands, but Grainger's sense of justice was skewed.

"Oh, him? You don't have to worry about that guy. I caught him visiting Iris's grave one day, admiring his handiwork. I've already taken care of him. He won't be bothering anyone else." He turned his attention to Cody's injured leg. "Do something with that leg. You're getting blood everywhere."

Cody looked at his thigh. There was a small stream of blood oozing from the wound, which meant the bullet had missed hitting a major blood vessel. He reached over and grabbed a shred of the mattress cloth he had torn earlier and tied it around his leg, applying pressure to the wound. Movement beyond the basement door caught his eye.

He could make out a small figure lurking in the shadows. The figure drew closer to the door and stepped out of the shadow. Maggie. *What is she doing? She should be a mile away by now.* His heart raced as he tried to think of a way to keep Grainger from seeing her.

"Who was it?" Cody asked to distract Grainger.

"Doesn't matter now. He won't be hurting anyone else." He waved the gun in a blasé manner.

"Did he say why he did it?" Cody knew what Grainger's reasoning was, but maybe finding out the original stalker's reasoning could help now. Anything to keep him talking.

"She rebuffed his attempts to ask her out. Said he was going to make her his, one way or another." Rage flared in his expression before a cold calm replaced it.

"You know, I think I'll go hunting. Go find me a little Magpie, bring it home, and pluck its wings. Let you watch. But first I need to make sure you can't get away." Grainger smiled, but before he could take a step in Cody's direction, Maggie hit him over the head with something, sending him to his knees. His gun flew from his hand and skidded across the room. Cody jumped from the bed and dove for the gun as Grainger tried to crawl for it.

They reached the gun at the same time. Panic propelled Cody forward. He couldn't let Grainger get the gun back. He swatted the gun away from Grainger, who sat up and threw a punch, catching Cody in the eye, sending him to his back.

Grainger straddled him and closed his hands around Cody's throat. He used his hands to beat at Grainger's arms, but he only squeezed tighter. Desperation caused him to act out of instinct, clawing at Grainger's hands. Cody needed to think smart if he was going to save himself and Maggie. His lungs begged for air, and his vision dimmed.

Cody maneuvered his arms under Grainger's and was bringing them up to break his grip when Grainger roared and let go. He stood and charged at Maggie. She had something in her hands. He heard the click and saw the barbs and wires discharge from the Taser she'd taken from Grainger's belt.

Cody's mouth went dry as Grainger grabbed her by the throat and lifted her off the ground. Either the probes had missed, or Grainger's adrenaline made the Taser ineffective. Her fingers clawed his hands as they continued to squeeze, and she tried in vain to kick herself free from him.

Cody jumped to his feet, ignoring the pain that radiated from his leg and head. He had to save Maggie. Slipping an arm around Grainger's throat, he brought his other arm up to press on his arm, adding pressure to the windpipe. Cody's body tensed as Maggie stood there rubbing her neck.

"Run, Maggie!" he growled at her as he pulled Grainger back to the room where they had been held.

Grainger struggled against Cody but couldn't free himself. In one swift movement, Grainger slammed his fist back against the gunshot wound in Cody's thigh. Cody howled in pain and lost his grip on Grainger, giving him enough slack to pull himself free. He turned and threw a punch, connecting with Cody's jaw, and delivered a kick to his stomach, sending him tumbling into the room.

Cody watched in terror as Grainger raced down the hall after Maggie. He stood and took a step in the direction Grainger had run, but putting his weight on his injured leg sent him to his knees. *Lord, help me get to Maggie.*

He put his hand on the floor to give himself some leverage to stand again when he felt Grainger's gun with his fingertips. He picked it up and stuck it in his waistband before standing and hobbling out of the room. He didn't dare put his full weight on his crippled leg. He couldn't afford the time another fall would take. Each agonizing step toward the stairs had him wondering if he would make it in time.

He climbed the stairs as fast as his leg would let him. As he crossed the threshold of the basement door, he heard shrill screams coming from outside. He increased his pace, dragging his leg through the living room and out the open front door just as Maggie had described.

Maggie lay on the ground and Grainger straddled her, pinning her cuffed hands to her stomach. She kicked her legs and bucked her torso, trying to throw him off her but it was no use. Grainger landed a punch to her jaw and Maggie screamed in pain.

Cody saw red, and the pain in his leg receded as he reached for the gun in his waistband. He couldn't risk shooting Grainger with Maggie in the line of fire though. "Grainger! Stop right there."

Grainger stopped and whirled around, sitting Maggie up and positioning her between him and Cody, using her body as a shield. He stood her up and started taking steps backward toward the wooded area. Maggie had blood streaming from a cut on her cheek, and her face was pale with fear. She had twigs stuck in her hair, and dirt covered her clothes, indicating she had put up a fight.

"Let her go!" Cody took slow steps in their direction, keeping the gun aimed at them, finger patiently waiting next to the trigger, waiting for a clear shot.

"That's not going to happen."

"Let her go, Grainger. You let her go and you can walk away."

"I'm not an idiot. I've had negotiating training too, don't forget that," Grainger yelled as he continued to take slow, steady steps toward the woods. Cody knew if they made it in to the woods there would be no hope he could catch them. His leg was on fire, and he was starting to feel the effects of blood loss. He needed to end this now.

"Grainger, I'm not talking to you as an officer of the law. I'm talking to you as a man trying to save the woman he loves. You can disappear into the woods, and we won't follow. I promise you."

"I don't believe you. If I keep her, I still have leverage." Grainger spoke from behind Maggie, not looking around her, never giving Cody a kill shot.

Maggie opened her eyes wide as if she had an idea, drawing his attention to her. Her eyes traveled meaningfully down to the ground on her right as she wiggled her right hand and subtly bent her elbow like she intended to elbow him, and then her eyes darted to the left.

He understood what her plan was and gave her a small nod. Using the fingers on her right hand, she counted down from three. When she got to one, she raised her cuffed hands and brought her right elbow back down, jabbing it into Grainger's stomach and dove to the left.

Cody took the shot, hitting Grainger in the right arm, sending him to the ground. Cody hurriedly limped over to where Grainger lay, clutching his wound and hollering profanities. He aimed the gun at Grainger. "Roll over onto your stomach."

"Are you crazy? You shot me. I could be bleeding out," he said through gritted teeth.

"You're not going to die from that wound. Now roll over or I'll give you a matching wound in the other shoulder."

Reluctantly, Grainger rolled over onto his stomach.

"Maggie, get the handcuffs from his belt and cuff him" She grabbed the cuffs from his belt and cuffed Grainger's hands behind his back. Without lowering the gun, he nudged Grainger with the toe of his boot. "Slowly get up."

Grainger rolled onto his right side and pushed himself into a seated position, then slowly got to his feet.

"Maggie, the handcuff key is on the key ring he keeps clipped to the loop on the right side of his belt."

Maggie unhooked the keys from Grainger's belt.

"It's the smallest key on the ring. If you'll find it, I'll unlock the cuffs. Grainger, walk to the house and have seat on the couch."

Grainger reluctantly shuffled across the lawn and up the porch steps. Cody followed behind, taking it easy on his leg.

Maggie walked up beside him and wedged herself under his arm, offering her body as a crutch. Together, they climbed the porch steps behind Grainger.

Cody unlocked the cuffs from Maggie's wrists and turned to Grainger. "Where are we?"

"I invoke my Miranda rights."

"Come on, Grainger! We've both got bullet wounds. Tell us where we are so we can get paramedics here."

He remained silent, staring at the open photo album on the coffee table. Cody knew he wouldn't be saying anything else to them.

"There's a phone on the kitchen wall. I'll go call 911. They'll be able to find us that way." Maggie walked out of the room.

Cody sat in a chair, watching Grainger. He couldn't understand what had driven him to such extremes.

"They'll be here as soon as possible," Maggie announced as she emerged from the kitchen. She sat on the arm of the chair, handing Cody several hand towels. She stuck her hand out. "Give me the gun."

He made the trade with her. After making sure the pressure dressing was secure on his leg, Cody hobbled to Grainger and slid a towel under his arm. He applied a neatly folded hand towel to Grainger's wound and tied it in place firmly.

Other than a quick inhale of breath, Grainger didn't react at all. He sat there, a defeated look on his face, his posture sagging.

Sirens filled the air minutes later. Cody opened the front door and went outside to meet the first responders. Maggie followed. He took a seat on the porch step, and she joined him.

"Not that I'm not grateful but what were you thinking coming back here?"

"Cody, how could you think I'd leave you? When I heard the gun go off and saw you drop from sight, my heart shattered. I couldn't escape and leave you here to die. So, I ran to the front of the house and quietly sneaked inside. Since Grainger had brought me up to the living room earlier, I knew how to get to the basement. Before he knocked me out, I was able to get the door unlocked, and he didn't relock it. I grabbed a pan off the stove as I passed through the kitchen. I stood at the top of the stairs and watched him push you back into the room."

"Maggie, you could have been killed." He pulled her into his tight embrace.

"But trapped down there, you definitely would have been killed. I love you, and I can't imagine my life without you." She pushed herself away so she could look in his eyes.

His reply was interrupted by an EMT. "Sheriff Smith, we need to get you to a hospital to get that leg looked at."

They were never alone after that. He wasn't able to tell her he felt the same way.

TWENTY-NINE

Maggie woke up and stretched the kinks from her back. It had been a week since her ordeal with Grainger. He'd taken them to his parents' place in the middle of the woods on the outskirts of town.

When the authorities showed up, Grainger and Cody had been taken to the hospital for treatment. She'd answered thousands of questions from different deputies before being allowed to join Cody. His wound was through and through and would heal nicely.

She'd been checked out since she'd taken two hits to the head in a short time. The doctors had confirmed a minor concussion but had given her an all clear. She had whiplash, bruises, and cuts from the ordeal. It would all heal.

Grainger had been patched up and taken to jail where he confessed to stalking her and killing Dee. He had lied when he told Cody he had disposed of Iris's prescriptions. Apparently, his original intention had been to kill Maggie by an overdose, like Iris. But he hadn't planned on Dee having second thoughts, so he'd had to readjust his plans.

Maggie had spent the last few days recuperating from the wreck and subsequent kidnapping. Amelia had dropped off three different meals and Jacob had been by her side most of the time. Babying her. Now she knew how he'd felt after his attack. They had agreed to take a week before starting the work on the house.

Today was the day they planned to start. He should be here before long. She slipped her feet into her duck slippers and headed down the stairs for her morning soda. She needed a jolt of caffeine before he got here.

Voices and laughter filtered in from outside. She looked out the kitchen window and saw several teenagers in a huddle. She walked out of the house and around to where they had been standing. Amelia was in the middle of the huddle doling out instructions.

"Amelia, what on earth are you doing here?" Maggie asked as she gave her friend a tight squeeze.

"Well, a little birdy told me you needed some help today, and since that awful deputy is behind bars, I thought it was safe for the kids to come out here now. We've got the primer, paint, and paint supplies. I'm going to have them start on the house."

"Would this little bird happen to be yea tall," Maggie held her hand above her head about four inches, "and wear a badge?"

"I've been sworn to secrecy." Amelia winked. "But if I'm not mistaken, that would be the birdy pulling up in the drive now."

Maggie turned to see Jacob's truck pulling into the drive. At the sight of the truck, she deflated. She'd really hoped to see Cody. They hadn't had a chance to talk since he was released from the hospital two days ago. He had been busy wrapping up the details of the case against Grainger, so she had given him space.

Jacob got out of the truck and walked to where she and Amelia stood. "Hey, sis. Where do you want me?"

"Um. See Amelia. She seems to have a pretty good handle on barking instructions." She chuckled and gestured over her shoulder to where Amelia had wondered off to show a teen the proper way to paint.

"Look, Magpie." He rubbed his hand across the back of his neck, a sign that he was nervous. "Can we talk?"

"Sure."

He led the way to the porch steps and gestured for her to sit next to him. "I didn't come alone. Cody's in the truck. He insisted that he sit down and talk with me before I came out here."

The passenger's side door of Jacob's truck opened, and Cody got out. The sight of him sent her heart galloping. He pulled a pair of crutches from the bed of the truck and positioned them under his arms. He leaned against the truck and lifted a hand in greeting while he waited for Jacob to finish.

She waved back. "What did you two talk about?"

"He told me everything. About how he'd been the one you were seeing. You know, when I talked to him that day, I'd never entertained the idea that he would be the one you were in love with. But looking back on it now, I can see it. I was being a macho big brother. If I had known, I would have beaten the crap out of him and then given him my blessing with the warning that if he hurt you the next beating would be ten times worse. But I didn't know it was him. And, obviously, I screwed things up for you both."

"I'm not going to lie to you, Jacob. What happened between Cody and I was very painful." She looked to where Cody stood. "I blamed myself for what happened. I thought there was something wrong with me. It wasn't until this past month, when he explained about your conversation with him that day, that I realized that wasn't the case."

"I'm sorry, Magpie. I never meant to hurt you. Or him for that matter. I promise never to meddle in your love life again."

She laughed and gave him a hug. "I forgive you. What kind of big brother would you be if you didn't try to protect me?"

"Good. Now go see that man. Don't make him wait any longer." He pointed at Cody.

"You're meddling already." She bumped him with her shoulder affectionately and sent him off to work before walking toward Cody. "You don't need to be here. You should be home propping up that leg," she scolded, a smile teasing her lips.

"Yeah, well, I wanted to talk to you, and since Jake and I had breakfast this morning and he told me he was coming this way, I thought I'd hitch a ride. Can we go inside?"

She nodded. Once inside, she sat on the couch. He sat next to her and took her hands in his. His hands were warm, and hers tingled at his touch. Using his thumb, he traced a line across the back of her hand.

"Maggie, I wanted to ask if we could try again. I know I messed up when I let you go but—"

She put her finger to his lips, stopping him in mid-sentence. "I know you thought you were doing was what was best for me. I want to try again; I really do, but you hurt me. I need to know that going forward you will let *me* decide what is best for me."

"Yes, absolutely." He leaned over and pulled a small box from his pocket. "I was going to give this to you that night. It was a promise ring. It was my promise to wait for you." He opened the box revealing the sapphire ring nestled in black velvet. "Maggie, I want to spend the rest of my life with you. I know that it may be too soon, so this is my promise now. I know that you've built a life for yourself in Houston. I promise to wait for you. I'll give you as much time as you need. I'll resign as sheriff, and I will move to Houston."

"I don't need any more time, Cody. I loved you then, and I love you now."

"In that case." He dropped carefully to one knee in front of her. He pulled the ring from the box and took her left hand in his. "Maggie. I knew from the first time I kissed you that I wanted to grow old with you. Then I foolishly made a decision without you. I promise to never do that again. I want to marry you. I want to place this ring on your finger and claim you as mine. Maggie, will you marry me?"

"Yes." A tear slid down her cheek. He slid the ring on her finger. She leaned forward and planted a tender kiss on his lips. "I love you, Cody Smith."

"And I love you, honey. I'm the luckiest man alive thanks to you, my Magpie."

KEEP READING
For a sneak peek at

JADED LOVE
By Jody Holford and Kara Leigh Miller

Chapter One

Kristy turned up the dial on the mini heater she kept under her desk. She ignored her buzzing phone and scrunched her brows as she re-read the lines she'd highlighted in the report. A headache blossomed at the base of her skull.

"Want a coffee?" Brianna asked as she walked past Kristy's cubical.

She looked up, smiled at her new coworker. "I'm good, but thank you."

"Oh, you have a heater." Brianna stepped closer, and Kristy fought the urge to lean back.

"A room full of scientists and we can't figure out the thermostat." Kristy laughed.

"Yeah. It's the building. I always dress in layers." Brianna shrugged and wandered toward the break room while Kristy mentally chastised herself for not having better social skills. She used to. But that was before everything changed.

Kristy flipped to the back of the multi-page document. Preliminary trials on a new blood pressure medication had gone very well. She'd actually been the one to open the file in the Chicago office almost twelve months ago. She'd been happy to take it over when she arrived at the New York office. But what she was reading didn't jive with the original results.

Several follow up trials revealed that lab mice experienced
signs of dizziness, vomiting, and loss of appetite.
In the most recent trial, 177/ 230 mice showed
one or both of these symptoms within six weeks of their original doses.

Lots of new medications often came with side effects, but such severe symptoms after several trials concerned her. Regardless of what the drug could do, pushing it forward didn't sound promising. She placed a sticky note next to the numbers just as Brianna returned.

Biting back a sigh, Kristy smiled and made eye contact. She couldn't avoid everyone.

Brianna leaned a hip on her desk as though they were old friends. "You settling in okay?"

"Yes. Other than it being cold in here, it's been good." Wracking her brain for a polite question, she asked, "What are you working on right now?"

Brianna tucked a strand of her brown bob behind her ear. The thick, black glasses she wore were somehow geeky and cool at the same time.

"A new sugar substitute. Looks good so far. It's into its fourth trial. It'll give people something to argue about other than the effects of aspartame," Brianna said.

This time, Kristy's laugh wasn't forced.

Brianna glanced at the clock on the wall. "I've got to get back to it. Let's grab lunch one day this week."

"Sure. That'd be great." The words left Kristy's mouth before she was sure if she meant them. She let out a deep breath as Brianna went back to her own cubicle. Thoughts of lunch with a colleague shouldn't make her insides twist. Hanging out with anyone other than her best friend Alessa and Kristy's family sent pinpricks of unease along her skin, although she didn't know why. Hanging out was normal, and she'd never been a hermit. She was still getting settled after her move and didn't have time for new friends. All excuses. But why was she making them?

Setting her coffee down, she told herself uncertainty about new people was normal. Caution never hurt anyone. Neither did a little faith. Maybe if she'd had more of both last year, she wouldn't have been taken. Pushing the thoughts of last year away took a lot of effort. She repeated a mantra in her head: *I am fine. I am safe.* The words took some of the edge off, but not all. Why couldn't she let herself trust that things would be okay? Maybe because she still hesitated over things like this.

"I'll go," she whispered the silent promise to herself. She'd go out and have fun with someone new. Maybe she'd invite Alessa. Needing to get out of her own head, the doubts over something so mundane, she flipped open the file again. She read through the entire document again before emailing her boss with her concerns.

* * *

Kristy leaned back in her chair and stretched. She glanced up at the clock, surprised it was already 5:55 PM. She'd worked through half of her emails—only to have another dozen show up—and made her way through two straightforward files. Her phone rang, and she was happy to see Alessa's name on the screen.

"Hey, what are you doing?" Alessa's voice was loud in Kristy's ear but made her smile. She'd missed Alessa when she moved away and was glad to be back in the same town.

"Just finishing up some files. You?"

"We just got home from the ultrasound."

Kristy smiled, picturing Alessa's face, giddy with excitement. Her friend had been through so much and deserved the happiness. She knew what Alessa was doing with the silence, and it made her laugh. "Are you going to tell me?"

Alessa giggled. Actually giggled, and Kristy leaned forward on her desk trying to imagine the last time she'd felt so much happiness. For herself.

"Nope. I'm actually not."

"You're such a tease." Kristy laughed. A couple of colleagues waved on their way out, reminding her of the time. Listening to Alessa talk about how she wanted to keep it a surprise but wasn't sure if she could, Kristy eyed the folders she still wanted to get to. Hesitating, she finally shoved them in her bag.

"You heading home?" Alessa asked.

"Yes. Do you need anything?"

"Actually, Josh has to go back to the clinic for a bit, so he's going to drop me at the church. I'm trying to organize the door prizes and decorations for the singles' dance," Alessa said.

Kristy shut down her computer and pulled on her jacket. Her phone beeped when she held it in the crook of her neck and for a moment she worried she might've inadvertently hung up on Alessa. But then Alessa sighed, signaling she was still on the line. "You want help."

"I'll bring food." Alessa's voice was sing-songy, and Kristy rolled her eyes. But her stomach growled at the same time.

"You know the way to my heart." With her bag and purse slung over her shoulder, Kristy waved goodnight to the few people still testing and reading. Brianna waved, a friendly smile in place. "I'm leaving now. See you soon." Kristy said a quick goodbye before tossing her phone into her purse.

Once on the subway, Kristy tried to ignore the smell of the large, dripping sandwich a man was eating two seats behind her, and instead let her thoughts wonder to her personal life. Why was she so reluctant to reach out and widen her social circle? She didn't want the answer to be related to what she'd endured with Raymond, the disgusting jerk who'd kidnapped her, knocked her around, and planned to do all manner of horrid things to her as a way to get back at her best friend. She shuddered thinking of him, seeing his face in the recesses of her mind. She pulled her purse tighter, hugging it to her chest as the train jostled her forward in her seat.

She'd put all of that behind her and had much to be grateful for; she didn't want the memories bogging her down or holding her back. She needed to move forward. Swallowing down nausea, she stood at the next stop. She definitely needed to move forward, away from the smell of that man's sandwich. The church wasn't far from the subway.

Because the silence of the quiet street was too much for her, Kristy spoke aloud, to herself. "See, Mom. I'm spending all of my time at church." Maybe not for praying, but she was doing well, hanging out with a friend, and she enjoyed feeling like she was part of something. She'd never envisioned herself spending so much time in a church. But, she had to admit, aside from being with her friends, which brought her a sense of calm, being there gave her a sense of peace. A freedom to let go of negative thoughts and worries. Or maybe that was because Alessa kept Kristy so busy helping she didn't have time to obsess.

Letting herself in, she inhaled the scent of vanilla candles and wood polish. Kristy unbuttoned her jacked and walked the aisle. The sound of Alessa humming in the room Pastor Ethan, or Ethan as Kristy called him, used as an office filtered out to Kristy. She smiled. On the other side of the church, there was a sitting room that led to a large rec center area where they held dances, special events, and receptions. The size of it still amazed her.

"Hey you," Alessa said. Standing at a fold up table loaded with an assortment of goods, her best friend smiled warmly. The gesture pushed away Kristy's earlier concerns.

"Hey yourself." Kristy embraced her, and then looked down at Alessa's protruding belly, unable to contain her grin. "I say boy."

Alessa laughed. "Why's that?"

Taking off her jacket and tossing it and her purse on the small loveseat in the corner of the office, she scanned the table. "Because there's a fifty percent chance I'm right."

"Very scientific, Dr. Andrews," Alessa said, mock seriousness in her eyes.

"I do what I can. These things look great, but I believe you promised food." Kristy looked around the office. It was homey and quaint, no doubt thanks to the added touches of Amanda, Pastor Ethan's wife and Alessa's sister-in-law.

"And I always keep my promises."

Alessa walked behind the desk and pulled out a small cooler. Her hair was tied up in a ponytail, and her youthful face reminded Kristy of when they had met in high school. So long ago, and yet, nothing had changed between them. Regardless of time, distance, love interests or vengeful psychos, their bond had always held.

Alessa unloaded the cooler onto the dark, heavy-grained wood. Kristy laughed at the bounty of food. Egg salad sandwiches, grapes, carrots and dip, strawberries, cans of soda, and of course, chocolate. Kristy opened the container of strawberries and popped one into her mouth.

"What? My appetite has picked up." Alessa snagged a ripe strawberry.

"I'll say. Not that I'm complaining. Being around you while you're pregnant means I'll never starve."

They opened the sandwiches and sat on the desk to eat before getting to work. Kristy played with the tab on the soda can for a moment before blurting, "I don't really need more friends. I have you guys and Amanda and Ethan. Brianna's nice, but maybe work should just be... work."

Alessa took a bite of her sandwich. "Brianna seems nice. And you spend a lot of hours at work so even if you don't want to be friends outside of your office, it doesn't hurt to have someone there you can go to or count on. What's the big deal about grabbing lunch?"

"I don't know." Kristy shrugged, not sure she wanted to get into it. Even though she'd opened the conversation by telling Alessa about the invite when they'd spoken earlier, Kristy no longer wanted to talk about her overly friendly co-worker.

"You'd tell me if you weren't okay. Right?"

Kristy looked at her friend, who glowed with pregnancy. Alessa had married Josh right after the ordeal with Raymond. She'd put herself back together, one beautiful piece at a time. Now she was having a baby with the man she loved. No traces of trauma, of flashbacks, or nightmares. She'd embraced her faith more since being with Josh. Or maybe since finding him.

"I'm fine. Stop worrying about me."

"Can't do that. Sorry. It's in the best friend handbook. Worry about bestie becoming introverted is right after must always bring ice cream in times of need." Alessa smiled around a handful of chocolate almonds.

"Hmm. I saw the ice cream, and fully support it, but must have missed the other. And, I'm not becoming introverted. I'm busy. I'm settling into a new job, a new apartment, a new life. I see you and Josh and Ethan and Amanda all the time."

Kristy took her wrapper to the garbage and began sorting through the goodies on the table. Gift cards, chocolates, books, and movie tickets were just some of the choices.

"You get all of these donated?" She glanced over her shoulder to where Alessa was leaning back on the couch, still watching her with concern in her pretty, brown eyes.

"Yes. The community is very supportive. Kristy, it happened to me, too. You can talk to me. I *want* you to talk to me."

Busying herself by separating the more expensive prizes, she ignored the tightness in her chest. "I'm fine, Alessa. And it happened mostly to you. I was just collateral damage. He was after you, not me. I should be asking you if you're all right, but it's pretty clear you are."

Tears stung her eyes, and she didn't look over when Alessa came to her side.

"You're who Raymond took. Yes, I was the reason, and I live with that every day."

"Alessa, that's not what I meant." Kristy turned to her, blinking away the tears.

"I know. But it's true." Alessa's voice was low. She put a hand on Kristy's arm. "We all have lingering feelings about what happened. But I have Josh, and I feel like you have no one to open up to."

"I have you." Kristy gave a watery smile and went back to her task.

"But you won't talk to me."

"Because nothing is wrong." Before Kristy could apologize for snapping, the door of the church whooshed open and thudded closed.

Alessa checked her watch. "Josh isn't due yet." She frowned.

Kristy patted Alessa's hand. "I'll go check."

Leaving before Alessa could answer, Kristy let out a shaky breath. She was fine. Or she had been, until she locked eyes with the man who stood in front of her. Easily over six feet tall with dark, mussed hair, he stared at her with a scowl on his face, his eyes narrowed. His gaze moved over her, traveling all the way down, then back up to lock onto her eyes again. His expression didn't soften one bit as he took a step forward. His bulky jacket made him look bigger, wider than he probably was, but it was his attitude and the way his eyes seemed to see everything at once that made the space seem smaller, airless. Electric. Kristy waited to feel fear or anxiety at the sudden appearance of a stranger, particularly one with such a sneer on his face and a presence that tangled her tongue.

"Is Ethan around?" His eyes were alert and pensive, but his voice sounded like he'd just woken up. Raspy. Thick. Handsome. The thought surprised her as much as her reaction to him had.

"No."

He arched an eyebrow, waiting, but no way was she saying more than she had to. The quickening in her pulse made it very clear she was overtired and not in full control of her judgement.

"Do you know when he will be?"

"No." She shook her head for emphasis. His lips quirked slightly. Then he looked past her to where Alessa stood in the doorway.

"Ethan will be back in the morning. Is there anything we can help you with?" Alessa asked, apparently unfazed by this man's presence. To be fair, she did have a good-looking, loving husband of her own. Or maybe pregnancy had made her blind. Could that happen?

"Thanks. You ladies shouldn't be here late at night by yourselves. Anyone could walk in." He looked back at Kristy.

Kristy stifled her laugh, thinking he wouldn't appreciate it, but arched her own eyebrow at the statement. Before he could say anything more, Alessa spoke, stepping toward them.

"My husband is due any minute to pick us up. Do you want to leave your name? I can let Ethan know you were here. He's my brother-in-law."

"And it's not that late," Kristy said, her tone almost defiant. Heat rose to her cheeks when Alessa gave her a funny look.

"I'll catch Ethan tomorrow. Please don't stay here much later by yourselves. It's really not safe." His gaze never left hers.

Kristy and Alessa watched him leave. When Kristy pulled her gaze away from the door, Alessa grinned at her. "What?"

Alessa laughed and turned back to the office. Kristy followed her, awareness and irritation fighting inside of her. "Oh nothing. Hot man got your tongue?"

"Shut up," Kristy said, making Alessa laugh harder.

"That's mature."

"Do you want to get this done or not?" Kristy started wrapping and labeling door prizes while Alessa selected items for a gift basket.

"Bet you'd meet him for lunch," Alessa said a few minutes later, breaking into another fit of giggles.

Kristy threw ribbon at her and smiled. "No. I wouldn't. I don't need more friends."

"Honey, you weren't looking at him like a friend."

Her throat tightened, but she kept her smile firmly in place. "I don't need any more anything. How about that? Let's finish this before Josh gets here."

Alessa let it go, and Kristy was grateful. But later that night, after Josh and Alessa had dropped her off at her apartment, she wondered if she had lied to her friend. Maybe she did need more. Want more. The problem was, the thought of admitting that sent enough fear to the pit of her stomach to push the thoughts far away, like she did her nightmares.

ABOUT THE AUTHOR

Jennifer Pierce currently lives in Arkansas with her husband and two children. She is a member of American Christian Fiction Writers and River Valley Writers, where she serves as secretary.

Connect with Jennifer online at:
lovereadwriterepeat.wordpress.com
Twitter.com/JennPierce82
Facebook.com/JenniferPierceauthor

Made in the USA
Middletown, DE
24 June 2018